GW00858155

SANCTUARY

To:
Mother, B.V.M.

LORRAINE MURPHY

SANCTUARY

AN ALBATROSS BOOK

© Lorraine Murphy 1992

Published in Australia and New Zealand by
Albatross Books Pty Ltd
PO Box 32, Sutherland
NSW 2232, Australia
in the United States of America by
Albatross Books
PO Box 131, Claremont
CA 91711, USA
and in the United Kingdom by
Lion Publishing plc
Peter's Way, Sandy Lane West
Littlemore, Oxford OX4 5HG, England

First edition 1992
Reprinted 1993

National Library of Australia
Cataloguing-in-Publication data

Murphy, Lorraine
Sanctuary

ISBN 0 86760 181 7 (Albatross)
ISBN 0 7459 2434 4 (Lion)

I.Title

A823.3

Cover illustration: Michael Mucci
Printed and bound by The Book Printer, Victoria

Contents

1

Million-dollar commercial

I COULD NEVER FORGET my sixteenth birthday.

Waves shimmered like raw silk as the yacht glided along, motor purring softly. The barefooted sailors had set out the luncheon on the back deck. But even in the shade the Mexican sun beat down fiercely.

It was the first of April.

A perfect birthday for a fat April fool.

I had decided to use the ladder. I felt quite calm. It hung off the back of the yacht and was never taken up. Tonight, maybe after midnight, I'd come on deck. The awning would hide even my huge bulk if anyone were on the bridge. Five steps down into the warm, salty Sea of Cortez. . . the dark waters closing in. . . Easy. . . no blood or pain like the other times. . .

Sanctuary. . . sanctuary. . .

'Jennifer Rich Morrison!' My mother's voice, teasing, silvery, but the steel underneath. She lingered over that middle name. 'How many of those tacos have you eaten?'

I glanced over my shoulder, across the gleaming pearly whiteness of the deck. Crimson awnings stretched against the sun, waves like blue diamonds — not a glimpse of land in sight. Spicy delicious smells of Mexican food lingered. My mother's long tanned legs were stretched out on the deck chair, Captain Morales standing attentively before her. Dad was stiffly upright, drink in hand.

Picture-perfect cruise: I remember thinking what a million-dollar commercial we would make.

We had about five minutes before the world blew up.

2

Whoosh!

'NINE.' I NIBBLED on my tenth taco and shrugged indifferently. I hadn't really wanted the last two, but I knew it irritated my mother.

'*O diez, no se,*' I said, practising my high school Spanish on the sailor who was collecting the dirty dishes. He was about my age, maybe a year or so older, with high Indian cheekbones and a slender body. A gold cross hung around his strong brown throat. He glanced at me now, a steady look with no hint of a smile.

'What? What's *diez*? Nine? Or ten? Oh, Jennifer!' There was an edge of shrillness in my mother's voice. 'Look at her!' She turned to my father. 'She's gobbling all that fattening Mexican food' — her own lunch had scarcely been touched, she was on another diet — 'and look at the sight of her! She's so fat, it's *obscene!*'

My father shot a swift look at me, then turned

away. One look was about all he could stand. He took a couple of deep swallows and the dark rum slopped over the edge of his glass.

'*Oye, Capitan!*' the sailor steering the boat called. I could see him motioning impatiently, but the awning blocked Captain Morales' view. It was obvious to me that the captain was anxious to join his crewman, but my mother continued to hold him there, commanding his attention. He smiled courteously, but his eyes were cold.

'*Momentito*, Esteban!' he called up and, if she'd taken the hint, perhaps he could have reached the bridge in time. Perhaps.

But she loved an audience too much; I writhed inwardly as she spoke to a complete stranger about my many faults. 'So stubborn. . . so fat. . . only five feet two inches — I'm five eight. Of course, our hair's the same colour. . .' We both had thick, wheat-coloured hair, but I'd whacked mine off the very first night aboard.

In the background I could hear the sailor call something in Spanish. But at the same time my mother was saying, '. . .and she has my lovely skin, but that weight — *gross!*'

Suddenly my father lurched to his feet. He understood Spanish quite well, although he'd never bothered to help me learn it. His million-dollar business took him all over Latin America. Now he was white to the lips.

'Captain! Captain, did you hear him? The man at

the wheel — he said he was going to switch the auxiliary generator to the spare bank. Your auxiliary's petrol-powered, isn't it?' The captain's dark impassive face splintered as the words hit him. 'If any gas has leaked into the fuel tank. . . *No! Esteban! No!* One spark — the fumes —' he screamed. *'Don't do it!'*

There was a soft *whoosh* and the ship rocked a little; then a tremendous bursting like a gigantic firecracker. Sections of the bridge rained down on us. My father wavered unsteadily, then a piece of railing smashed straight through him and came out of his chest.

The bottles of liquor fell to the deck and bright flames shot through the floorboards. Liquid fires ran along the tequila, the rum and mezcal. Bottles exploded and glass sprayed the deck. Screams of incredible agony came from below — the rest of the crew had been there.

A sailor burst through the kitchen door, hair and clothes blazing, and stumbled towards me. The next explosion tore the ship in two. My mother and the captain fell straight down and disappeared and a bolt of superheated air struck my left side. The burning man and I fell backwards, over the railing.

Down into the warm depths I fell, turning over and over, my clothes a dangerous heavy anchor. I tried to loosen my ankle-high sneakers, but couldn't even bend to reach them, I was going so fast. I plunged through layers of blue and green into purple, deepening to black. The farther I fell, the colder it became. I was a thousand kilometres from the sun, a thousand years in the dark. My lips were clamped shut, my chest aching from lack of air. I tumbled and spun and lost all sense of direction.

It was there in the dark that the hand reached out and touched my face once, feebly.

In panic, I almost took a fatal breath, striking out blindly with both hands. My numbed fingers tangled in a jacket — it was the man who had gone overboard with me. I grabbed at him. His head swung limply and I knew he had very little time left.

Sharp knives of pain stabbed my chest. My ears were roaring and the lack of oxygen was making me lightheaded. Here was what I'd wanted for so long — sanctuary, death in the dark.

But the sailor was completely helpless.

And there was some stupid, stubborn part of me that would not let me die at his expense. One hand clamped against his nose and mouth, I clung to him with the other and kicked out frantically. Had I left it just too long?

But the sea released its hold. We burst upwards through layers of light into sun and foam and air that stabbed the lungs like sharp wire. We bobbed there in the waves, gulping and choking, his weight dragging at me.

In front of us, in the blinding sunshine, the beautiful ship made one final leap as if it could escape. But the sea that had let us go took it instead. Slowly,

slowly, it fell apart and the pieces sank below the surface. Ash and the smell of burning drifted towards us. We sank to escape the heat. And when we surfaced again, the ship had vanished.

We were completely alone in an empty sea.

3

Adrift

I SWAM, FRANTICALLY AT FIRST, and then slower and slower. His heavy body pulled me back. Bits and pieces of the wreck began to pop up around us. A long deckchair struck my feet on its way up and I snatched at it, but the waves carried it off. Tears of helplessness began to pour down my face.

Suddenly, with a smash of foam that made me scream in terror, the ship's railing surfaced, almost intact, trailing the small dinghy by a single rope. I hurled myself towards the dinghy with the last of my strength and seized the hanging rope, pulling us to its side. The rope parted from the railing and the dinghy came free.

I clung there, gasping, trying to hold the man's head up. Stabbing rockets of pain shot along my left side and the arm I'd clamped around his shoulder.

The noise of the explosion and the water in my ears must have nearly deafened me, because only then did I hear the cries. As the boat spun, I could see the young sailor with the gold cross swimming weakly towards us.

'Here! *Aqui* — here!' I shrieked. Then I saw that he was trying to pull someone. I yanked on the rope and kicked towards him. The most expensive swimming instructors in the most expensive summer camps in the world had tutored me but, hampered as I was, I could make no headway. A hopeless failure in everything. . .

We drifted away from the only other people in the world. I didn't dare let go of the rope. Swimming in pools had taught me nothing of waves or current. Maybe, if I could get into the boat — perhaps there were oars?

Never had the weight I carried been more humiliating — I could not get myself over the side of the boat. Sobbing, I swam alongside, pulling the sailor, my legs kicking helplessly. Low as the boat was with water, I could not get in and my arms were becoming too weak to hold on much longer.

I hooked the rope under the sailor's arms and wrapped the end around the rowlock. The next wave lifted us up and I jumped, striking my forehead against the seat. Legs flailing in the water, I held on with both hands, half in, half out. I knew I must get in. Must get in, or I would fall back into the sea. And this time I would never come up. I pulled myself hand over hand along the seat, my left side and arm a white fire of agony. The dinghy tipped dangerously, but I swung my leg and rolled at last into the bottom.

I struggled to sit up, leaned over and somehow hauled the sailor in.

He was dead.

It had all been for nothing. He'd probably died right after he'd reached out to me. Anyone else would have saved his life, but he had only me to depend on. Wrapping my numbed arms around myself, I knelt there, limp and exhausted. All for nothing. Another failure to add to the long long list.

'*Oye!*'

I squinted into the sun glare. It was the swimmers. But they were too far away for me to help them.

Besides, what was the use? There was no land in sight. No way to send a message. This was just a little dinghy. It was nicely fitted out, but useless except to die in, starving and burnt dry by the sun.

I had lived for a long time inside a ball of grey mist. I knew this ball existed only in my head, but in there it was quiet. Empty and quiet and very, very hopeless. For a few minutes I had broken out of the mist, and felt a breath of life, only to find that in the sunlight everything was just as hopeless. The words of my favourite album rocked through my head:

> Hope will creep and crawl away,
> Death calls louder, day by day.
> We've lost all the wanting,

Only hear the taunting —
Do it, do it, let go and die. . .

Across the water I heard the sailor shout again. Still alive, but sounding weaker now. Their last chance — and maybe mine, too.

Clumsily I scrabbled for the oars and laid one in the rowlock. The second oar almost slipped from my painful left hand. I caught it in time, my heart pounding.

'Oh God!' The words burst out, stupid and meaningless. What 'God' did I mean?

As I started to pull towards the men, the boat swung and jumped in the waves. I could barely see their heads in the silver glare. The oars were terribly heavy. I pulled with all my strength. It seemed like hours before I heard a cry. . . I'd nearly run them down.

I leaned over to help. The young sailor lifted the one he'd been towing; I grabbed him, almost lost him, got a handful of hair. He was sinking, but the pain must have revived him because he flung himself forward and I pulled him in.

The younger one got halfway in and had to be dragged the rest of the way. I did it awkwardly, only one arm working properly, and he screamed once as his body hit the floorboards. He fell on his face.

The back of his shirt was gone, his upper arm charred black. Bits of skin fell off in flakes and liquid oozed from the edges. I wrenched my eyes away and turned to the man he'd been holding all this time. He was breathing, just barely.

We lay there, shaking with chills, while the afternoon sun burned the backs of our necks. My clothes hung wet and clammy.

The world I'd lived in had disappeared. I hadn't liked that world very much. Fat, ugly, stupid, I'd wanted out. My wish had been granted.

The wilderness islands in this area were uninhabited — even if we could reach one. No-one knew we were here; we hadn't passed a ship for days. Certainly there'd been no chance to send an SOS.

A dead man rolled at our feet. I couldn't even speak their language properly. Anyway, they must despise me as they despised my parents — rich foreigners who spurned their land, hired their boats, then got drunk, ate like pigs, ordered them around.

I knew nothing about steering a boat. A trip to study nature? What a laugh! The hot sun was making my head ache. A chunk of hair seemed to be missing near my forehead and my ear felt as though it were on fire.

Why was I here, anyway?

I'd come home just — when? — a week ago, to my mother's implacable face and Another Wonderful New Plan.

'We're going on a cruise, to get some sunshine, my darling,' she'd announced. No discussion. Typical of her to arrange my life as coolly as she arranged the furniture. The luxurious apartment was my mother's pride, redecorated every six months. 'An *environmental* tour, of course! The newest thing!' She laughed mockingly. 'You're the "Save the World" freak! You'll love Mexico!'

'I'm not going,' I told her sullenly. 'My mid-term exams are coming up next week. Anyway, I like the cold weather.' I did, too. All fat people like cold weather. They can wrap thick coats around themselves and pretend they're invisible.

'And I've got tons of gorgeous clothes for you,' my mother went on, as if I'd said nothing. 'Enormous, extra-large sizes, of course,' she added with malicious regret.

This time I'd hold out. I *would*!

'Go by yourself! I won't!' I screamed. And then, trying for control, I continued more quietly, 'Let me go to Gran's. I'll study and. . .'

My mother's lips thinned. 'Oh, no, not Grandmother's. Your father knows how I feel about her. And so does she. We're *going*.'

I'd snatched my books and run into my bedroom. That at least had always been my own. But I'd stopped, appalled. Closets open, drawers hanging, all empty. All my favourite shirts, pants, even the new white birthday sweater from Gran. Everything gone from my sanctuary. I went back to her.

'Where is everything?' I tried for steadiness.

'Everything?' She looked up archly, enjoying playing games with me. 'What do you mean?'

'My clothes.' Calm. Keep calm.

'Oh, *those*. Well. . .' she drew out the words tantalisingly. 'I bought you some decent things.'

She danced to the hall closet and carried out dozens of boxes, opening them with what seemed like genuine enthusiasm. You couldn't tell if she was putting on an act sometimes. She was that good. The clothes came tumbling out. Expensive things. Beautiful silky nightgowns — I always wore pyjamas — bathing suits, high fashion even in the huge half-sizes I needed. Brilliant glowing colours. But nothing I would ever want to wear.

I was humiliated to tears. 'I'll look like a green and yellow elephant!'

She'd hummed to herself, ignoring me completely, and held up a pair of stone-washed jeans.

I looked down at those jeans now. I'd worn them daily, leaving the others untouched. I'd show her. She'd wanted me to get a tan, so I'd deliberately stayed in the shade. And now my skin would have no protection at all. I'd burn and blister and peel in the open boat — an uncomfortable way to die. Thirst and hunger and burns dripping pus. Better to go before that.

I moved quickly. My right foot was over the side and I was following it when he opened his eyes.

'*Agua*,' he whispered through cracked lips.

Shamed, I yanked my foot back. Sunk in my own dark thoughts, I'd forgotten the sick men entirely. But I shook my head to show bewilderment and lifted my hands.

He pointed with his chin to small lockers under the oars. I opened one. Water sloshed in the compartment as well as at our feet. Doubtfully I examined the cans inside. Yes, there were some with fresh water. I unscrewed the top and let the warmish liquid trickle over his face and lips. Slowly I poured the water into his mouth.

Finally, he turned his head away. I took a small sip, then another. I couldn't remember anything so delicious in my life. My hands shook with the effort not to gulp down the whole thing, but I forced myself to turn to the other man.

'*Mi hermano*,' he said.

'Uh, your brother?'

He turned and stared at his brother's face. Large round tears rolled down his cheeks and he made no effort to wipe them away. Nor did he seem at all ashamed to have me see him cry. He must really love him a lot, I thought. We said nothing for a full minute. Then he moved and a low moan broke from him. Was it the salt hitting his wounds or the shock wearing off?

I searched through the lockers for something, anything, to ease the pain. There was a small medicine kit with some stuff jumbled in it. I held up tubes of antiseptic lotion and he nodded. 'Mister, do you have the faintest idea what your back looks like? This is probably for sunburn!' He stared at me without comprehension.

I squeezed a tube and poured lotion in my hand.

At the first touch he shrieked and slumped unconscious. His shoulder was red-raw meat. I clamped
my mouth shut as I wiped the stuff on and covered
the burns with bandages from the kit. It was hard
not to vomit.

I smeared some more lotion on my own burns,
whimpering as I did, then fitted a life jacket under
his head. Now the brother. Still curled up like a little
foetus, he hadn't a mark on him. But the pulse in
his throat was very, very slow.

I was desperate to relieve myself so I used one of
the bailing buckets. I was glad neither of them could
see me and gladder still to dump it in the sea, rinsing
the pail before they woke up.

Every time the dinghy moved, the dead man
moved, too. The burned sailor had not even
focussed on him and that was good. The body was
stiff already and horrible to touch. I wrapped a tarp
around him, then realised we might need it and
unrolled it again. It seemed heartless, but every
single thing that might help us (Help us? What a
hopeless idea!) must be saved.

From time to time I glanced at the horizon; sunset
was not far away. I remembered from even those
few days on the yacht that there was really no
twilight in this part of Mexico. It was day and the
next thing you knew, it was pitch-dark. Scrounging
hurriedly, I found boxes of hard biscuits, more water
cans, metal buckets, rope. Maybe there were flares?
Ships on television shows all had flares. But the last

locker was blocked by the dead body. I didn't even know the poor guy's name.

The boat moved gently with the current, but I had no idea where it was taking us. There was no map, no compass. What would I have done with them, anyhow?

I sat exhausted for a few minutes and then got to work. Closed the dead sailor's eyes. His clothes were worthless — just pieces of material stuck to his skin. Before he went overboard, I tried to think what they did at sea burials. Weights on the feet, wrapping in a flag — well, those were things we didn't have. But I couldn't just dump him out; he wasn't a piece of meat. He'd been a person.

I had no belief in God. Gran, long ago, had taught me prayers. She'd never said they were magic, but I'd prayed night after night that somehow I could go and be with her. It never happened and I stopped believing then. Oh, a few times I'd thought of trying again. There was a teacher who cared. One of my shrinks had some compassion. But nothing changed. And after that I quit.

But I said a few words over the crewman. 'God, if there is anyone out there, please take this man. He died a rotten death. Give him a break in your other world — if there *is* another world.'

I pushed and pulled the stiffened form to the front, then slid him over the side as quietly as I could. There was hardly a splash. The boat bounced and spun, lightened of his weight. He turned over and over in the waves and tiny luminous glows shone all around him. Otherwise it was utterly dark.

For one terrible moment I thought something moved through the water. Had I brought sharks to follow us? Was Jaws or another monster out there? There was no-one to ask. I trembled and sweated in the mild air until I saw that his body was gone and the phosphorescence was, too.

When the shivering ended, there was only exhaustion. I stared emptily out into the night. The boat rocked and creaked.

Beautiful Mexico. Glorious cruise.

'I'll have the wild life sounds all taped. . . Camcorder, get me the best for nature's *wonders*. . .' The waves lapped against the boat and I recalled my mother's sarcastic tone. Nature's wonders. Sure. 'Have some ghostwriter slob to put it all together for me. . . book circuits. . . Save the Environment!. . . TV spots. . . I'll be the Green World's spokesperson. . .' That's all it had meant to her. And now. . .

I leaned forward on the hard seat and all my thoughts drifted away like smoke.

4

Land

THE SAILORS' MUMBLING AND GROANING woke me. I was stiff and sore, sneakers chafing my ankles. Everything glowed in silver. It was the most terrifying sight of my life — cold moonlight, empty, empty sea. I trailed my fingers in the waves slapping our boat. Warm. This was the night I'd been going to climb down the ladder, just let go and sink. Why not now?

My clothes were wet and disgusting. I had to use the bailing can again. In all my life I'd never been so uncomfortable. Morning would be worse. The men would die. There was no hope.

Yet I hesitated.

The two men lay absolutely helpless. If I stayed . . . I crawled over to look. Alive, both of them. Moaning, little *thunk-thunk-thunk* in their throats. Alive.

I crept back to my place and slept instantly.

When I woke, it was dawn. The sailor was trying to get the outboard started. It must have been agonising: sweat and tears poured down his cheeks; his teeth were clenched. He sank back with a groan.

I struggled to my knees and crawled past him to the motor. He'd been attempting to wipe off the salt. I rubbed the sides with my sleeve and looked at it. It seemed to be full of fuel. Hesitantly, I jerked the cord. No response. Maybe it needed something else to start it? Yes, this motor had been made in the United States and the word 'choke' was on it. I moved the switch to 'choke', pulled it a couple of times.

Nothing.

The sailor opened his eyes and touched his chest. 'Juan Jose de Gonsalvo.' His voice was weak.

I pointed to myself. 'Jennifer Morrison.'

He tried it. Hard for him to say Jennifer.

'Try Jen.'

'Jen.' He smiled. Our hands went out together, clasped firmly. But instead of letting go, he turned my wrist so that the scars showed white in the sun. There was compassion in his face.

I yanked my hand away. 'Who do you think you are. . .' and stopped, furious. Who did he think he was to feel sorry for me? A Mexican who'd just joined the unemployed, burned down to the bone so badly he'd never make it. And he was sorry for *me*?

I started to cry. Crying is something I don't allow myself to do. But once begun, I couldn't stop. It went on for a long time. I trembled and my eyes stung and I had to wipe my nose on my sleeve. He waited and watched. I'd get control.

Think of my mother, so beautiful, so beautiful — couldn't I have reached out, just a little, to her? She'd loved life so greedily; how could she have been expected to understand someone who hated it so much? I remembered the flames, the screams. . . and then I'd begin crying all over again. When I'd gulped and hiccoughed and finally pulled myself together, his head was nodding. In a minute he was deeply asleep. His brother lay motionless.

I took out the water can and moistened their lips. I swallowed a few gulps and shook the box of dry biscuits. My stomach was growling. I could have devoured the whole box. I took one cracker, then guiltily two more. I tried to chew them slowly, but it was no use. Quickly, I shoved temptation back into the locker.

I kept my mind off the food by busily dumping water out of the boat bottom. As I wiped the engine once more, the fog lifted and long golden bars of sunlight glittered across the sea. It was morning.

With new hope I positioned the choke and tried again. Nothing. Maybe I was being too gentle. I checked. The switch was off. Pulling like an idiot, with the engine switch off!

Stupid, stupid. Just what they'd all told me. Too dumb to live! I ground my teeth in despair.

On the third try it started with a roar, so loud that

Juan Jose was shocked awake and I fell backwards. What if I exploded it like the ship?

But the roar continued and, by Juan Jose's motions, I guessed it was enough to ease the choke back. Gently. The roar softened and became a purr. Then we started around in circles. Finally, I discovered that the metal bar was a kind of steering device and grabbed it. Juan Jose pointed to the sun and, as the boat straightened, waved me ahead.

I nodded. 'Aye, captain. Sun on the right, north is ahead.' He gave me a gallant thumbs-up.

We chugged north.

After a while I reached into the locker and got out the water and crackers for him. He nibbled listlessly and then pointed to the locker.

'Put it away?'

He nodded his head.

'Think it's safer there?' My voice trembled with anger. Did he think I'd eat them? I could have and he'd never have known.

He looked troubled. Maybe he wanted to save them in case something knocked us over? Suddenly nervous, I began looking in the water for signs of Jaws. When he bit that fishing boat in two. . .

'Sharks?' I asked him and my hands shook. I couldn't think of the Spanish word. I made big biting mouths, then sliced my hand like a fin cutting through water.

'No,' he shook his head, but his eyes avoided mine. Then there *were* sharks!

'*Terra*?' He looked puzzled. 'I mean. . . *tierra*, land. Are there any islands . . . *islas*?' He nodded and pointed north.

I persisted. '*Personas*? I mean *puebla*. . . no, no, that's a city. . . *la gente* — doesn't that mean people? I'm so stupid! Trying to steer and talk a foreign language at the same time! *La gente*?'

Juan Jose had been watching me anxiously. He shook his head. Did that mean no people or he didn't know?

He pointed north.

'I know, I know,' I said irritably. 'I know which way! What's there?'

He looked at me sadly. '*Pájaros. Isla de Pájaros.*' He flapped one hand like a bird and then shut his eyes.

Pájaros. Birds. Birds on an island. No people? But at least if we could get to an island, light a signal fire, roast the birds — then we could travel on to the next island, and the next. . . surely we'd find some-body?

I steered the little boat all morning till my hands grew sore on the bar. And all the time I kept wondering how long this fuel would hold out. The heat increased as the sun rose.

I peeled off my long-sleeved blouse. I was afraid it would blow overboard, so I shoved it under a coil of rope; an hour later I added the sneakers. My feet were white and stiff when I pulled the wet laces loose and yanked off the heavy things.

On my ankles were round sore spots that itched like crazy. I didn't dare to dip either my feet or my sneakers over the side. Who knew what might be gliding along underneath us? I sloshed around the water in the bottom of the boat. And soon that was gone, sucked up by the sun.

The sea glittered so that my eyes watered and squinted. Yesterday's headache was back. I felt the burns on my scalp as the sweat hit them.

The sun beat down and beat down, the men slept, the boat moved steadily north. Lulled by the heat and motion, I was half-asleep when the motor began to cough and sputter. We bucked and bounced and drifted to a stop. Out of fuel.

I just sat there for a minute, stupefied. Then I crawled forward to scrounge through the lockers and found a spare fuel can. It was the only one.

I had it uncapped and ready to pour when Juan Jose's urgent 'No. . . no!' stopped me. I rescrewed the top. Stupid — stupid! Hot engine — and I'd been about to add cool petrol!

Without a breath of wind, we drifted in the sun, waiting for the overheated engine to adjust. I was grateful for the small protection of my T-shirt. I wondered idly if that was what the young seaman had done. Tried to switch from a half-empty to a full tank — showing off a little, not knowing that a single spark could explode a hot tank. Especially when there was not the smallest breeze to blow away the fumes. One single mistake. . .

While we waited I rigged up a kind of shelter for the men. At last the fuel could be poured in. The smell of it reminded me of the look of horror on the captain's face before he died — before they all died.

And here it was the next day. I was hungry and thirsty —and hot. Every few minutes I scooped up a handful of water and poured it over me. It dried just as fast and the salt that was left itched horribly. Finally, I pulled off the damp jeans and laid them in the bottom of the boat. With the long T-shirt, I had as much on as the ladies at the fancy cabanas at Cozumel, maybe more. Anyway, Juan Jose was asleep again, or at least his eyes were closed. We went on, endlessly.

And suddenly, there was land.

'Made it! We made it!' I screamed aloud.

Juan Jose woke, dazed. Automatically, he reached out to touch his brother, gently. How strange it would be to have someone care for you like that.

The island was not very large. Maybe fishermen came here. Maybe otter catchers, like on the *Island of Blue Dolphins*. No, no, don't think about that, I said to myself. The girl in that book was alone for twenty years!

As we came closer, I lost heart again.

There were tall cliffs along this side of the island. Really tall. Impossible for anyone to climb, even with equipment. My hopes began to fade. Small caves worn out of the rock were barely visible, but so shallow that they were all under water.

I tried to hug the shore, steering cautiously around submerged rocks. There was an unpleasant smell of burning that warned of an overheated engine. Frantically I examined the shore, circling the whole island, but there seemed no possible way to get on it. The outboard started to buck; we were close to stalling.

In desperation I ran us closer to the caves again, peering in to see if there were any holes we might climb through, up to the beach. Juan Jose cried out sharply — I'd come dangerously near the rocks. Then he slumped forward.

The sun was directly overhead and blinding, the caves deep in shadow. Yet as we swept past, I thought I'd glimpsed movement in there. Swinging the boat around, clumsily, I sent us again towards the biggest cave. From its depths came a sound like a cough, a dangerous rumble. Something gleamed in there — eyes? I caught my breath, almost ramming us into a rock. Then we were past. There in the hot sun I felt sick and very cold.

Something was in that cave. The boat stuttered on. At the only possible approach to the island I burst into tears of rage.

'Oh, no! Oh, no! Look at it! Broken rocks, no sand; we'll be smashed if we go in!' It was Juan Jose, much weaker then, who dragged himself to the front of the boat. His shoulder was red and black — he must have been in agony. With his good arm, he directed me to the right, where the boulders looked worst.

But after all, he should be the expert.

So I aimed us at the spot and came in over-cautiously, almost stalling an engine that smelled badly scorched. There was a narrow crack between huge rocks; we crept along till we came to boulders that seemed to wedge us in. Only seemed to, because the boat kept bobbing up and down. There was nothing to tie up to. I didn't have the faintest idea how I could get ashore — for two sick men it would be impossible. I waited, hearing the motor grinding unpleasantly.

'*Zapatos.*' He pointed to the sneakers. I scrambled into shoes and jeans while Juan Jose opened a locker and fumbled with coils of rope. I shut off the motor and the silence rushed in.

The rocks were wet and covered with a green slime as slippery as ice. I threw boxes and cans, buckets and the tarp as far up on them as possible. Some of the things slid down the other side to splash in water. Low water, I hoped. Finally, there was nothing left. Inching forward, I took the rope from the sailor's hand. His eyes filled with tears of helpless frustration. We could have cried together because try as I might, the rope wouldn't catch on anything.

Hopeless.

Without giving myself a minute to think, I pulled the rope around my waist and leaped for the nearest rock. Missed, of course, and fell between two others. I climbed along them, grateful for the tough material protecting my legs. There was no coral, you could tell that much, but the stones were rough and grey, with green stuff clinging to them. Reaching the top, covered with green filth, I dragged the cord over and around the rocks and pulled the boat towards me hand over hand.

If Juan Jose had not helped, it could never have been done. But time was running out — it was then or not at all. Judging the waves, he made a jump and teetered on the rock's edge. I grabbed for him and we fell together, hitting his shoulder so that he screamed.

For a few seconds we lay gasping and sobbing, then struggled back for his brother. Somehow we got him to shore.

We dragged each other along. My hands were strong enough, but my unexercised body was exhausted before we'd gone more than a couple of steps. Between us we crawled and rested, crawled and rested, so that twenty metres seemed to take us hours. The heat was awful and there was not a shred of breeze.

At last we gained a stony beach and rested again. Birds were hopping all over the place. They moved away from us fast enough, across stones and a little dirty sand. They didn't look as if they'd be easy to catch. Juan Jose pointed out the biggest and bossiest ones. They were gulls — he knew the English word — black-and-white with bright red beaks.

Wearily we staggered up the hill, the sailor groaning and wobbling badly by this time, his brother a dead weight between us. A small outcropping of flattened rock offered some shade and there we stopped. Flat above and below, two could lie down or three could sit.

'At least it will keep off the rain.' He stared blearily. '*Lluvia*,' I added.

'*Lluvia*, no. *Septiembre*.'

'Oh, no, you can't mean that it won't rain till September? It's only April!' Suddenly he took a half-step and sank forward on his face. Barely catching the brother in time, I lowered him to the ground and ran to Juan Jose's side. He was unconscious again.

No-one to help me. What was I supposed to do?

We needed the tarpaulin, the medicine chest, all the stuff. I couldn't do anything without them. Most of all the boat, our lifeline, had to be pulled up on shore.

God. *Why me?*

Puffing hard, I shuffled back, perspiration soaking me from head to foot.

The boat was gone.

5

Swirling dust and feathers

A GIANT HAND PUNCHED ME in the chest.

A thief? Someone hidden on the island? Something in the water?

Then I saw it bobbing gently, far out beyond the beach.

We *had* to have that boat!

Madly, I tore off jeans and sneakers and plunged across the slippery rocks. It was impossible to dive because there might be submerged boulders and no way to get into the water except to slide down these three metre stones. And little help I'd be with a broken leg. But I moved as fast as possible to the place where we'd come in. An end of frayed rope hung limply.

I flung myself into the sea.

It was amazing how fast I moved away from the

beach. The swimming lessons that cost thousands must be paying off! Only, as I swam, the boat moved farther ahead. I swam as hard as I could — for our lives! But the boat moved faster.

Finally, I trod water and looked back. And got my worst shock since the ship had blown up. The island was almost out of sight. Even treading water I was being swept away. It was a current and I was in the middle of it — a powerful, swift-moving river in the sea. I could never catch the boat because the current would keep it just ahead of me. But I would not be able to get back to the island, either, and so I would die here.

Well, but that's what it all came down to, wasn't it? Just sinking down, letting go. . . letting go. . .

But the traitor body refused. Kept fighting, legs pumping, arms flailing, lips closed against the sea. I had to get back. Had to save. . . who? Juan Jose? His brother? *Me*? I fought like a crazy person. Mindlessly, against my own desire to let go.

Just barely able to see the top of the island, flat little thing that it was, I struck out towards it. The tide was very strong and I was bone-tired. In twenty-four hours I'd done more physical activity than in my past lifetime. My heart, layered in fat, would never take the strain. Wearily, I forced my arms to thrash in the direction of that unobtainable shore.

It seemed a very long time. And when I dared to look, I wasn't any closer. Soon it wouldn't matter; too exhausted to raise my arms, I began to gasp. . .

let go. . . let. . .

It was then that the heads popped up. Right in front of me. Heads!

I opened my mouth and shrieked. Salty water rushed in — the whole ocean. I choked, sank, fought desperately to the surface.

Nothing there.

What had I seen? Imagined? Crazy — I was going crazy!

With the faintest of ripples they appeared again — six of them this time. Goggly eyes, sleek hides, whiskers. All around me, about three metres away.

Seals. No. Sea lions.

Suddenly there were other heads — a dozen or more, all watching me with care. They knew I wasn't one of them, but what was I?

One of them flipped over on his back. Immediately, four or five others imitated him. My shoulders were aching. I flipped myself over. Easier. Able to catch my breath. I lay puffing and grunting, seeing the island coming a little closer. The sea lions floated with me. Did they ever come as far as the beach?

I turned right side up and began the journey again. Stroke. Stroke. An old *Mr McGoo* cartoon flashed into my mind — he's so nearsighted he thinks a union suit in a washing machine is a swimmer. He jumps up and down, yelling, 'Good girl, Florence! Stroke, stroke!' I burst out laughing. Florence Chadwick swam the Channel: could I swim to the island? The sea lions accompanied me, grinning sympathetically. Every so often I stopped and floated a bit with them. It was easier. Tired to death, I looked up to see cliffs looming above me — too close, much too close!

Helpless, I was sucked in by the tide. I bounced off something, felt skin tear, struck again. Blood on my arms, blood in the water, trying to protect my ribs, my face. An infection would be fatal. An infection! I was being pounded to death and worried about infections!

I hit the beach with a tremendous final crash, vomited till my throat rasped, crawled farther up on the hot stones.

And slept.

It was cooler when I woke. So cool I was shaking. The sun would set and then would come the quick velvet dark. I stumbled over to the cans and boxes and few clothes, pulling as many as I could onto the tarp. I yanked and pushed it to our camp. The rest must be left till morning. Have to search the island tomorrow — find water, food, a place to build a signal fire.

The men lay just where they'd fallen. Both were curled up, both still breathed, but Juan Jose's bandages felt wet and oozing. Working as fast as I could in the fading light, I unwrapped the tarp and rolled them on it. They shivered as the ends were folded around them. Maybe they'd be warm enough, side by side. Anyway it was pitch dark and no more could be done tonight.

I was ravenous.

There were biscuits. It was agony to leave them untouched, but one wouldn't be enough. Not for me. I knew my pig-like qualities very well — I'd finish a box. I turned away, searching in another box for something else. Anything!

I found some long chewy strips and nibbled, wary of their saltiness. It was some sort of dried salted meat. I was so used to gulping whatever I ate that it took a while to manage the stuff. Gnaw off a chunk, let it soften in your mouth, chew. Slowly. I fell asleep, still grinding on it, and woke up half-choked.

Stars were blazing — millions of them. The sky was pure black and the tiny points glittered. Not all were white. There were blues and greens up there. The air was dry and mild. Arms under my head, I lay on my back and stared for hours. Twice I saw shooting stars. Probably the worst was over, I assured myself. Things would be better in the morning, rescue ships or something. People would come to save us. Turning drowsily, I fell asleep.

In the dawn light the two figures were motionless.

Dead, both of them. I fell back, sick with misery and despair. And hidden within, a sneaking feeling of. . . relief. Now it was my turn.

It should have happened yesterday. I thought pityingly of myself plunging into danger like a real fool, after a stupid boat. And yet. . . it would have been an easy way to die.

Only next time — this *was* next time — I'd let the current pull me out, out, far beyond any hope of return. To sink and join the other bones scattered on the floor of the welcoming sea.

Why not now? I shrugged. Why not? While the mist layered the world and before the cruel sun came. I pushed myself erect and shuffled awkwardly past the silent figures.

'*Dios!*'

I shrieked in terror, stumbled and almost fell. Who? What?

It was one of them, crying out to God in his sleep. Heart pounding, I scrambled over there and crouched above them.

They were alive — alive, both of them! In an agony of fury, I backed away. It wasn't my problem. I'd done enough, more than enough. Killed the first sailor with my clumsiness, dumped us all in this God-forsaken wilderness. I was through with all of it.

In just my T-shirt and underwear I slid down to the beach. Gulls and the other kinds of birds pecked at the ground or flew in aimless circles. Feet first, I lowered myself into the clear depths, splashing away the grittiness on my skin and hair, and paddled away. Milky grey haze lay on the water.

Just a few metres off, the shore became invisible. No voices or bells or people-sounds to tell where the land ended and the colourless sea began. Even that early, the Sea of Cortez was warm. I stroked evenly along, heading for the open sea.

'Jen-nee!' The call pierced the thick fog. I gasped, half-turning, and swallowed buckets of ocean. Gran? But. . .

'Come back this minute!' Only Gran had ever, ever called me Jenny. But it couldn't be! Maybe a bird? 'Jen-nee!' Yet it sounded like Gran.

I thrashed back to shore, ran madly up the little hill. Only the men lay there, heavily asleep. No-one to answer. No-one.

Shaken into a dreary, hopeless weeping, I went back to the shore and fetched the supply boxes up to our camp. Gran would have helped these men, just as she'd helped people in the camps. The survivors.

Finally, the tears stopped. I was all cried out — I, the one who never cried! I was as limp as a broken doll, but there was water to search for, these guys to help. I dragged on the wet sneakers, stumbled down to the tiny beach and up a farther slope. I must have looked ridiculous, but the birds made no comments.

I was starving. Longingly, I remembered break-fasts of melons and eggs and beans on board ship. A little basket always sat in the centre of the table. It looked like a sombrero but, when you pulled off the top, the inside was full of soft warm pancakes.

Before long saliva was dripping on my chin. All my thoughts were food-thoughts: that last lunch with thick tomato slices, guacamole salad, taco chips. I was a person who'd always been fed and cleaned up for. We had a maid, a cook. And now I was supposed to take care of a couple of helpless men?

Abruptly, I remembered people.

My mother, her laugh like silver bells jangled. . .
Once, hair all powdered with snow, she'd come back
late from the opera to find the maid at her wit's end
with my whiny five-year-old self. Rocking me back
to sleep in her arms — I'd forgotten that! — singing
the arias with her flushed cheek against mine. . . and
an autumn day. . . my dad carrying a very small Jen
on his shoulders, drifting red and gold leaves caught
in his sweater. . . we'd been a family, then. How had
we lost it all? Just a flash, gone as quickly as it came.

A different lifetime. And people who were history.

A bird's squawk roused me. I'd crushed its egg;
sharp edges stabbed through my shoe.

There was a path here, a very clear trail where no
brush grew. The birds' nests were just scattered
bunches of twigs, the eggs sand-coloured. No
wonder I hadn't seen them. I sat and yanked off the
broken pieces of shell. Immediately, the birds
quieted. Some returned to their camouflaged nests.

The bird with greyish wings, whose egg had been
squashed, flew up and down helplessly. The captain
had shown us slides each night about the islands
we'd see the next day. I'd ignored most of them, but
it seemed to me that the blackwings were
Heermann's gulls and the white and grey were some
kind of terns.

The contents of the egg drained into the dry thirsty
soil. Eggs. Invalids had eggs.

Strange about the pathway — it didn't look as if it had been made by animals. People, then? Did people ever come here? My heart began to beat heavily. The sun had risen and the heat was already intense. Sweat trickled down my back. If people came, we'd be saved. There was a sudden vision of a creamy white ship out to sea coming to carry us back.

Back to what? A world of money. There'd always been plenty of that.

A world empty of parents. Friends? None.

And what did I want in that world?

The answer came quite clearly. To be dead.

I sat tiredly for a minute longer, then climbed the few remaining steps to the top. A valley stretched below, with snow in it. Snow? No, but something white — a great, enormous open place like a square, surrounded by the brown vegetation of the island. I stared in wonder.

They were birds. The birds on the hillsides were nothing. Those were the loners, the isolates — like me. I had a sudden memory of standing all alone, while groups of classmates talked and giggled at a great distance.

This square was jammed with birds. Dust and feathers swirled in the air, bird screams, sudden flights, sudden returns. A huge vertical stone offered a bit of shade to huddle in. I stared and stared. Without binoculars it was impossible to see clearly but, wherever I moved, the solitary birds screeched and flew up and the others all followed suit.

Finally, I duck-walked to the nearest shade, a big rock. And then the next, moving slowly closer and closer to the square. Fat thighs chafed against each other and my stomach couldn't stand the pressure. But when I moved crouched double, birds were not so disturbed.

I got as near as I dared, sank down and watched. I felt mesmerised by the sight. They were always in motion, it seemed. Inside the square were two different kinds of terns. Some of the birds already had chicks; others sat on eggs. After a while I recognised couples — they traded places on the nests. I didn't take my eyes off them. They lived here and they survived. They must know where the water was and they found food. And became food themselves.

I quickly saw that the outer perimeter of the square was made up of the Heermann's gulls. Bigger, stronger, noisier than the terns, they acted like robbers and murderers. The first time a Heermann's gull scared away a tern to devour its egg, I jumped to my feet. The birds scattered, but soon were back. The tern cried piteously and the gull finished off the egg without concern. And the gulls ate chicks, too.

At first it was so horrible that I couldn't watch. The beautiful nature specials on TV never showed things like that. They'd all shown how animals and birds live together in peace. Only people bring death. At least, all my teachers agreed on that — human beings, mostly those in the United States, all cause wars and destruction.

The terns weren't able to fight off the gulls. Only the ones way inside the square were safe. They were bigger, more mature. Or maybe they were more experienced.

And then I saw another side of the gulls.

Right out of the sun, a swarm of birds came winging in from nowhere, like missiles. Big as gulls, they had bright yellow feet. They stabbed the chicks, pounced on eggs. I was up in a second, but there was no need. The Heermann's gulls, squalling and cackling and battering with their wings, rose up like pilots defending their homeland.

They swirled around the yellow-footed gulls to peck and rip. Encouraged, the terns flew into the fight, adding to the racket. The noise was unbelievable. The enemy attackers fought a bit more, but finally retreated to wherever they'd come from.

I stood and cheered. Somehow, it was inspiring to see the birds defend their teritory so gallantly. Then, suddenly, I realised how long I'd been watching them, fascinated. I pulled up the front of my thigh-length T-shirt, and began piling eggs into it. How could I have wasted so much time?

Every messy nest had just one egg, so I knew I was taking that mother's only child. But I had to do it. The men would need something nourishing, and that meant eggs.

I skidded in my usual clumsy fashion and broke three eggs on a slope, before learning to dig in my feet. Better the eggs than my neck. The strange path began again just this side of the slope and it was easier walking. I located more eggs — gulls', this time — and shut my ears to their parents' cries.

When I got back to the beach, it had disappeared under a wall of water. I stopped short, almost losing the eggs. Waves were pouring in from the sea, covering the place where we'd come ashore.

The whole flat place was a lake.

Whitecaps swished around my feet, rising higher as I watched. The water couldn't rise as high as the birds' square or they'd never survive there. But it would block me from our camp for long precious hours.

The men waited, hungry and thirsty. But it wasn't my problem — not my business. My mother would have agreed.

'Oh no!' she'd trilled scornfully whenever I'd appeared with my picket signs. 'Another protest for the poor, poor migrants? Jen, you haven't tasted a grape in years! Or are we throwing blood at nuclear reactors today?' Her mockery held me dumb in silent fury. 'Little rich girls with their guilt hanging down to their $200 shoes! When do those overpaid instructors have time to teach lessons?'

Useless to remind Mother that *she'd* been the one to insist on the glitzy, ultra-expensive school.

'Heavens — you've got problems enough — that weight, your pricey shrink. . . why get involved? Mind your own business!'

Yes, my mother would have approved. Sit down,

wait it out. . . who cared?

Anger burst like a rocket in my brain, bringing me unsuspected strength. I leaped up and took a step forward.

6

Broken eggs

IT MIGHTN'T BE DEEP YET. I took a chance and waded in, tightening the shirtful of eggs. Only up to my knees at first, not too bad, but with a nasty kind of undertow. I started across carefully.

In the middle, the water was around my thighs, but I was still moving, only a little slower. I could feel a pulling at my feet. Not the water; more like mud, sucking. I had just a few yards to go when one foot caught tight. Then the mud or sand or whatever clamped shut. My other foot was gripped as if in a vice.

It was some kind of quicksand.

I went into a total panic — screaming, thrashing, trying to lift my legs. One would come loose and then the other sank deeper.

I clung to the eggs till I realised both hands were needed for balance. With bitterness I let them drop into the roiling mess. Not all of them fell out of sight;

some lay on top, others could be seen right under the surface. My right leg suddenly came loose. Almost overbalancing, I leaned forward and the left yanked free. A few eggs still floated in front of me. I forced myself to stop struggling and breathed deep. But not to yell — there wasn't anyone to come.

It's close. Very close. You can make it to shore. One foot. One foot. Don't fall. Immediately, I fell.

Beating madly at the water, I was sucked down faster, faster. Oh God, *God*. . . help!

With the most tremendous effort of my life, I went limp. The drag eased.

Slow. Move the arm. Easy. Talking to myself. . . crazy. My legs floated up. Not a lot, but now it was more like swimming. I dragged handfuls of mud towards me. Gained a few inches. A couple more. My left ankle touched some hard object — a rock? Pressed down on it. The ground became firmer. Home free.

I crawled out and lay face down on the dry hot sand. The water must not come this high — it was as arid as any desert. I beat the ground with my bare hands, sick with shock and hunger and fury for the lost eggs.

But not for long. As I staggered to my feet, I saw a nest without a parent and put the egg in my soaking, muddy shirt. I found eight more, scaring away the bird to steal each one. Four others were in nests that looked abandoned. Like latchkey kids, the eggs were at risk. If it wasn't the yellow-legged invaders, it was me.

As I neared our camp the sound of crying became audible. Long, gulping sobs: a man in pain. I stopped, pulled back a little, shouted. He'd hate to have me see him like that.

He was silent when I arrived, but his eyes were feverish. Around his mouth, the skin was pulled tight. He looked haggard.

Carefully I unrolled my shirt and laid the precious contents on the ground. No plates, of course. I broke four eggs into a tin cup and stirred them with my fingers, then offered it to him. He stared with awe at me, then at the food. I smiled with the pride of actually doing something on my own, something that required brains and guts.

But his admiration was not all for me.

'*Huevos!*' he breathed, '*huevos ma. . .* ' I couldn't understand the rest. *M*-something. My Spanish was awful.

'Sure, eggs. . .uhm, *huevos*,' I repeated. '*Huevos* but not cooked.'

Mah-hee-something. He didn't smile, but he drank it all, reverently.

I shrugged. *Mah-hee* was beyond me, but breaking up the rest of the eggs was not. One turned out to be not an egg but a half-formed foetus. I flung it away in disgust before I remembered that everything here was food. Everything.

His brother couldn't be wakened to eat, so I drank the raw eggs without a shiver. I could have swallowed dozens more. They had a sort of fishy smell, but the liquid was soothing to a throat scratched dry from screaming. And they filled a part of the empty hole in me.

Juan Jose nodded over his cup. As I leaned towards him, there was the most appalling smell — a sweetish, rotting scent — that must have been his wounds.

I burned with shame. Sitting there watching birds while he cried in agony. His shoulder should have been tended hours ago! When he finished the eggs, I gave him all the water he could drink. I was supposed to have searched for water, too! Helping him to shift over on his side, I tried to peel off the bandage. It was stuck. Skin and blood came with it and yellowish gunk.

Medicine chest, water, clean cloth — it would have been better to have had a pail heating up water in the sun. Why hadn't I thought of that before? I hauled back a couple of buckets.

No matter how carefully the burns were touched, it was a horror. Juan Jose held himself in place, but he screamed in anguish. Dead skin, pus in the folds, raw flesh. When the worst parts had been cleaned, I poured on some of the green ointment, rubbing a little on my burned ear, and spread my blouse lightly on top. When I rolled him back, he was grey and sweaty, eyes wild with pain. He'd screamed so much he had no voice left at all.

Even more frightening, his brother never stirred

and Juan Jose hadn't noticed. He just looked up at me like a sad, sick animal. I poured four aspirins into him and waited to see the effect.

He grew drowsy almost at once. As his head nodded, he forced his eyes open and pointed to my clothes. I raised my eyebrows. He lifted a finger towards the sun, traced a line on my arm.

'My clothes? Put them on? All right, all right!' I was irritable. Maybe he was worried about sunburn; more likely the sight of me was disgusting. But I was not going to wear that heavy junk. Finally, he slept and I could sneak off.

Our water supply was dangerously low. Lying down in the small shade would have been glorious, but there was a spring to find and the quicksand lake to avoid.

But the lake was gone. I tossed stones onto the swiftly drying ground where salt filled the open cracks. Still damp, it was easy to cross.

When were the salt flats covered by the sea? I had to find out. And a spring — we desperately needed water, eggs, birds to eat. Raw? There seemed to be no scrap of wood here and the only bushes were thin, too brittle for a real fire — even if there were matches.

It wasn't till very late afternoon that I found the spring. If it was the only one, we were in trouble. Shallow, hidden beneath a heavy overhang of boulders, it was a trickle. The pail had to be held at arm's length to reach it and it seemed to take hours to dribble down. And then I drank it as fast as it filled in long delicious gulps. Full at last, me and the bucket, I started back.

Dummy! Why hadn't I brought another pail for eggs? I took off the T-shirt and carried it over my shoulder, putting down the pail each time there was a cache of eggs. There were hundreds on this slope, but the shirt was about ready to split. I collected ten.

There was a list of things to do and no way to write them. Gone was the cute little bulletin board near my desk with a fat pink pig on my notepad in a bedroom that existed somewhere on a distant planet.

The tide returned as I reached our ledge and the waters rose noisily behind me. Half-dazed with tiredness, I forced water and egg into a sleepy Juan Jose and swallowed my share out of the shells. Not enough. My stomach clamoured for potatoes baked and smothered in butter, a thick steak. The brother refused to open his mouth, but if I held his head down and pulled out his lips from the side, he swallowed quite a lot. I finished the rest.

I tried to focus my exhausted brain. . . get more eggs tomorrow. . . signal fire. . . with what?. . . I curled myself on the still-warm rocks and was instantly asleep.

I woke suddenly and completely. The birds were very noisy. Perhaps their dawn signal? Their cries of 'ke-e-er' and 'tsear' echoed to our side of the island. Lying there, stiff and hungry and thirsty, I watched the last stars wink out. God, shutting off the lights.

Who'd said that?

Another memory — long ago, when I'd still been allowed to stay with Gran. Maybe I was five or so and woke early, like this, to see her at the open window. I'd crept out of bed and we stood watching the morning come. What were the phrases she'd quoted from the Bible. . . 'Till the dawn star rises. . . on the wings of morning. . .' Couldn't remember, but it had been cool and peaceful, my fingers in the old woman's big hard hand. I'd believed, then.

A feeling as if tough elastic bands around my chest had been cut through. . . the air was sweet. . .

'*Oye!*'

I sat up. The birds were making a tremendous racket, but it had really sounded like a man's voice. I looked over at the two sailors. Juan Jose's eyes were wide open, sunken like black holes in his face. His body was taut.

I heard the sound of a boat hitting stone.

It wasn't my imagination! The birds knew it, too! I opened my mouth to yell with joy, but the sailor's hand flashed up in a *Stop* sign. I scrambled to him, a huge grin stretching my lips.

'Rescue time! We're sav. . . ' His hand clapped hard over my mouth and his head shook in warning. He looked feverish, but not delirious. What was the matter with him?

'*Huevos. . . huevos. . .*' he croaked.

'Oh, eggs? You want eggs?' He must be really sick. They'd come just in time. 'Sure, but first let me call the men!'

His eyes grew wilder, despairing. Something was very wrong! He dragged me down and we were flat on the ground as the first of the men tramped past. Shells were crushed under their feet and fledglings, too. We heard the dying cheeps of those that couldn't get away fast enough.

We lay almost without breathing, listening to dozens of feet go by. Without understanding anything, I was gripped with terror. Juan Jose was just as still, ear pressed to the ground, a long trembling through his body.

There were gleeful shouts as they reached the top, more yells when they came to the square of birds. And then the screams of the birds began. Before had been nothing — now it sounded as if they were being killed! But that couldn't be, because I saw them, clouds and clouds of terns and gulls, rising and swooping over us and back again to where the men were. And we heard a *thud-thud-thud* sound as heavy clubs struck the ground.

What hellish thing were they doing? Because it *was* a hell. . . the invisible men cursing and laughing, the birds crying. Finally, I couldn't stand it any longer. Juan Jose had sunk back into his half-daze. I began to crawl along the ground, scraping more skin off my bare knees.

I couldn't see the square from here, but the path was visible.

The men were there. Their clubs rose and fell, rose

and fell. They were smashing the eggs. Parent birds flew in helpless circles. Some of the eggs had hatched; chicks tried desperately to scramble out of the way. But the men paid no attention and their thick sandals crushed living birds left and right. Dark blood dripped over the rocks, eggs spilled in streams that were sucked up into the earth. I hid my face.

The birds that were so beautiful! The eggs that Juan Jose had treated with such awe! Why would they destroy them? It made no sense! And why was I so terribly afraid? Suddenly a man appeared on the near side of our camp. He hammered the heavy stick about, searching for hidden eggs. And there *had* been some on this side — I'd gathered them only last night. He was a heavyset man with a wide moustache; his white trousers were splotched with red that was already drying.

I waited too long. When I did move, he saw me. How could he help it? A huge white elephant in a flapping T-shirt, having trouble just lurching to her feet, then falling on the scattered pebbles. Without a word, he lifted his club and ran straight at me.

I sprawled over backwards and my fingers came down hard on one of the spiny little pincushion cactuses. The pain was so frightful that it hurled me into action. I rolled sideways and came up fast, driving the spines in even deeper.

I ran.

Stupidly, I started back towards our camp. In a

second I realised that there was no help for me there. And the sick men would never be able to escape. So I swerved to the far side of the hill. One glance backwards showed no-one else in sight. But it was not a matter of stopping to explain — the man held the club expertly above his head. If he threw it, I was finished.

Why was he after me?

In this light he could tell I was light-skinned, too fair for a Mexican — possibly a tourist. Why didn't he stop? I began to weave back and forth, to throw off his aim, but it slowed me down. If I hadn't been so terrified, I'd have thrown myself on the ground and begged for mercy. I hadn't *done* anything! And I couldn't go much farther — my side ached. My breath came in gasps.

Abruptly, I was on the very edge of the cliff. Looking down, I could see only the wild rushing waters around the caves we'd passed on the first day. In the loose gravel, my feet skidded and chunks of rock tumbled down into the foam.

The awful drop was sickening; desperately, I turned back towards my pursuer. Again my foot slipped and I hurled my weight into the cliff edge, scrambling for any kind of hold at all.

He'd been too close. His hand had been reaching for my hair, intending to drag me back or push me over — I will never know. Because his knees struck my prone body, he overbalanced and his own momentum drove him ahead. His club dropped near me and his wide hat flew off. He went over the cliff without a sound and fell like a stone.

7

Very real terror

I CRAWLED TO THE EDGE and vomited. There was nothing in my stomach, but I vomited again with horror at his death. Weak and wobbly, I staggered to my feet, impelled by sheer blind terror. A man had tried to kill me. Others might. Bent over as low as possible, I stumbled back to our rocks.

The hope of rescue was as bitter as the vomit in my mouth. These men must live not far away. If we ever did escape and came into their towns. . . I slid the last few metres on my stomach. Luckily, there were no nests close by. Perhaps the searchers would overlook us. And just yesterday I'd been angry that there'd been no easy eggs to pick up around here!

Juan Jose roused when I crawled into the narrow space near him.

He peered vacantly at me. *'Que pasó*?. . . what. . .?'

I lay flat, dragging in long sobbing breaths.

'A man,' I choked, 'he tried. . . tried to. . . ' I slashed

two fingers across my neck.

His eyes widened in horror. 'Where?' His head swivelled towards the path. His voice was too loud.

'Shh. . . shh. . .' I pointed to the cliffs, pantomiming falling over. He gasped.

A wild howl of fury rose from the cliff edge. From all directions came shouts and cries.

Shivering uncontrollably, I crept to the nearest mass of boulders and squeezed between them. A thought of snakes touched my mind, briefly. Wasn't this the home of the rattleless rattlesnake? I vaguely remembered one of the captain's slides. . . another girl had seen it in an air-conditioned lounge, bored, stuffed with food. A thousand years ago.

The men were standing on the cliff edge, looking down. One held my attacker's club. Would they think he had leaned over too far, dislodging a nest? Would they start a search near us?

No, they looked up at the sun, glanced around briefly and began shuffling down to the boats. I lay motionless, getting a clear view of a dozen or more men wearing loose white trousers and big hats, many of them barefooted. Very ordinary men. Impossible ever to identify any of them.

The last two were different. They walked slowly behind the others and examined the ground. My heart thudded. Had I dropped a scrap of cloth, left a footprint? They stopped quite suddenly, watching the men pile into the boats. Both were heavily muscled. One was taller than all the rest. They wore jeans instead of the baggy pants.

The tall one had a harsh strong voice. The leader, it seemed, because the other bowed and nodded, but said not a word. His speech was too slurred and rapid for me to understand, but his accent was different, too.

And then he took off his hat and his hair was as light as mine. 'An American!' I almost shouted. How stupid! All of us were Americans.

'Help us!' But my lips barely moved. It might be our only chance, yet I didn't dare. There was something vaguely repellent about him, for all his good looks. The arrogance of the way he stood, thumbs hooked in his belt, the submissiveness of the Mexican before him — the whole weird operation.

And then he laughed.

All around him lay dead birds and smashed eggs. One of his own men had disappeared and might be dead. His laugh echoed in this desolate place — casual, unconcerned, chilling. There was a deadly quality about his amusement, as if some human part of him was missing.

I shrank down. They finally left. A few men had waited till the two descended, sure-footed and silent. I wriggled out of the hiding place, wary as the birds, trying to keep them all in view.

Their boats sailed out beyond the barrier rocks. Dirty boats, none as big as Captain Morales', with nets on the sides. Their leader got on board alone; his boat was the biggest, red-and-black. No-one else

— he was both captain and crew.

What I could see was just a very handsome man, strong, tanned, blond. And yet the feeling of terror I got, only looking at him, was absolutely real. He glanced back once. I would not have moved towards him for anything in the world.

They sailed back and forth, back and forth, searching for the lost man. I stayed down flat, although the sun was baking me and the pain of the cactus needles was agonising. My back was itching madly; there were new, raw scrapes along my legs.

Finally, a long wailing cry broke from one boat — they had found him. In a grim procession they moved away and I was free to crawl to the sailors. The tarp I arranged as a kind of awning over them and then I sat to pick out the largest of the cactus spines. The men slept. I had no strength at all. Leaning against a big rock, I fell into a kind of doze.

It was after midday when the sun's glare woke me. Moving like a dreamer, I poured water down the men's unresisting throats, sponged them all over with sea water and replaced the tarp.

I trudged back to the valley. Where the beautiful white square had been the day before was a vast desolation.

The birds circled, crying, crying. I recalled Gran's Bible story — 'Rachel wailing for her children.' The birds sounded exactly like women mourning for their lost ones.

The ground was strewn with feathers and shells.

I picked up a few unbroken eggs here and there, feeling truly remorseful, for these eggs must be the only ones the birds would have this season. But we had to live, too.

I'd remembered the pail this time and filled it with the bodies of dead small birds, some still inside the eggs.

The old tired bewilderment filled me again. The birds were innocent. What was the point of a world where nothing at all made sense?

> Sick of life. . . it sucks,
> Sick of living, gonna die. . .[1]

Drearily I turned towards the camp. The old grey feelings of misery and deadness, which had retreated for a time, came back stronger than ever. The world was a rotten place.

Twice before I'd tried to leave. The razor blade time, I'd planned every move. Except for my father getting so drunk that he came home hours too early from the party and found me bleeding in the bathtub. They got me a shrink that time.

I'd waited.

The next try, it was a collection of my mother's tranquillisers, one at a time. I took them dreamily and floated calmly into the darkness. The stomach pump woke me. My mother's face glared furiously down at me; her evening had been ruined.

I rested for a minute and stared at the devastation.

There was very little water and what we had wouldn't last for three people till September. Most of the eggs were broken. Our chance to escape had come and gone.

Exhausted, I got up with the heavy pail and went back. The sailor's brother looked as if he were dying. That was all I needed. Fresh water into the metal bucket. In the broiling afternoon sun it ought to heat up quickly. Meanwhile I sponged the men down and broke the few precious eggs into a cup.

There was absolutely no reason to go on.

The birds I dumped into the water — it began to steam and smelled horrible.

Without me the sailors had no chance. Not my problem.

I stirred the pot of boiling things. I was so tired.

A faint memory touched me — Gran, stirring a pot of soup, smiling at me. Loving me. Thousands of miles away, but still alive. If we ever escaped, I would find her, live with her, learn to believe again. How I wanted to!

And then? Wouldn't she die, too? So what was the point?

I fed the 'soup' to the men. Disgusting stuff. In it was fuzz off the birds' bodies that couldn't be strained away. It hadn't really boiled, just got hot. Pieces of feet and eyes bobbed around in the sickening mess. Visions of food, real food, wavered in front of me as I forced it down. Pizzas with cheese, pastries and fresh rolls from the little 14th Street bakery, cherry cakes drenched in rum. I drank it, fed it to the men and told myself I would not throw up.

Amazingly, we all kept it down. Every drop was finished — I licked up the last part. Just as well. In this heat it would be putrid by morning. I dressed the sailor's burns; not much ointment was left. What could anyone do for him when it was all gone? I was distancing myself already; I no longer thought of him by his name. Just 'the sailor'.

Quite suddenly I was praying. The men slept quietly, lost in a dreamland that at least spared them more pain. I started to explain, then realised that God — if there was a God — knew all about it. So I stopped. But then I began again. What else could I do?

'I'm here and I don't belong here. I mean, the others all wanted to live and I didn't — don't. This is the third — no, counting the ship, the fourth time I should have died and didn't. So why have you kept me alive? Me, of all people? Is it for punishment? Starving is such a terrible way to die. And thirsting to death.'

I waited, but there was no answer. I dropped off to sleep sitting up.

The morning came and brought the day's only coolness. Stumbling down to the water, half-asleep, I waded out to my neck, scrubbing at my hair, cautious of my healing ear and pincushioned hand. Slowly the cactus spines were working themselves loose.

Mist lay thick all around and the birds called through it. For the first time there were dozens of fish nearby.

Could they be caught in just a bucket?

Frantically I raced back, grabbed the old plastic bailing pail and plunged too fast over the slippery wet rocks. Sliding at top speed right down between the two sharpest ones, I landed with the breath knocked out of me.

The fog parted a little and there was the boat. It was the black-and-red from yesterday, moving so quietly that it loomed up like a ghost ship. Had it been there before? Had anyone seen me? No movement aboard, except a dinghy swinging loosely, outboard motor on the rear and a tightly-wrapped sail on the side. Silent. Then a soft *chug-chug-chug* started up and the ship disappeared into the fog.

Finally, I dared to try for the fish. The first time I came up with a whole bucketful — and nearly dropped the lot. Nothing else had gone right, so why should this? But when one bunch of sardines was safely on the rocks, there was another, and another — five, six. Then nothing.

Sardines, salt water to clean them of sand — it was all dragged up on shore. The men lay quietly. They breathed, but very slowly, and their heartbeats were faint.

I'd wanted to dry the fish — save them for another day. Instead I cut them up, sloshed them around in a cup of fresh water and fed the men as much as they would take.

The pail of water began to heat on the sun-baked rock and I stretched out gratefully in the shade. My legs were cut and scratched, with a couple of large purplish bruises, skin gone from the sides of both knees. Across my shoulders and on my forehead was the itch of sunburn.

The soles of my feet were getting tougher; I no longer bothered with sneakers. The mound that was my belly had begun to shrink. Except for the constant nagging hunger, the thing that I missed most was that I'd never had someone to talk to.

'Why am I here? Oh Lord, speak to me — please!'

I waited, but there was no answer. Only the shushing, swirling noises of the water pouring over the salt flats. No light, no voice, not even an idea.

Groggy with the heat, I picked up the second metal bucket and headed for the spring, searching the ground along the way. A few bushes had little reddish berries on them, something like rose hips. They were tart and juicy: I scooped up every one in sight.

There were some green plants in the shade; I chewed the tiny branches, remembering the Nicaraguans fleeing through the jungle, and the woman saying, ' We'd stop on our way to Costa Rica and find tender leaves to eat.' They didn't satisfy, but they didn't seem to be poisonous either.

Moving like a sleepwalker, I picked up a few eggs and added them to the collection. The terror of the last days became a kind of hazy dream.

The rattler must have been lying on the far side of the rock. When I stepped over him, he struck upwards. But he only hit the pail and it tipped, scattering the bright red berries all over the ground.

What I felt was fury — red, hot and blinding. It should have been panic because, of course, it was the rattleless rattler; if he'd hit the big artery in my thigh, the poison would have pumped in minutes to my heart. But he hadn't. He'd missed and lost us all those juicy, precious berries, as well as the eggs.

I swung the metal pail with every ounce of strength and struck him behind the thick neck. He flopped a couple of times and fell motionless. He was food then, the same meat that specialty stores put up in neat little cans.

With a sharp rock I sliced off his head and nearly fainted when he twitched in my hand. But it must have been his death-move, because the blood flowed and he didn't. The berries were hunted down one by one and wrapped up in my shirt with the snake. The bucket was filled with water.

I stumbled back to find that nothing had changed. The sailors murmured sleepily. The berries were chewed very, very slowly; their tartness was savoury. With all the water I'd drunk at the spring, I almost felt full. Maybe the rest of the berries might be dried. I laid a few on flat stones while I yanked off the snake's skin — a messy job.

Sliced open, there was nothing in its belly. So I cut off thick chunks and threw them into the heated water. My mouth filled with saliva as I looked at the steaming can. A strange-looking mess, but it was life to us.

A screech distracted me. It was a yellow-footed gull dropping from nowhere to scoop away some of our berries. With a strangled yell I leaped to my feet, almost upsetting the stew, and flung a handful of gravel at it. With another shriek it flew off and I threw a rock, too late.

I recovered a couple of berries that had fallen, and sat down, discouraged out of all proportion. Anyway, the bird had only stolen a tiny bit. I hadn't knocked over the stew. How could I remember each second that everything here attacked or was attacked? We had survived. And I was the one responsible.

I reminded myself of that.

8

The glitter of binoculars

I MISSED THE SOUNDS OF MUSIC. And the songs I'd listened to most were a lot truer here on this island than in my clean and pampered life at home.

> Contaminated water,
> Mass starvation. . .
> Mutilated bodies[2]

All that was right here in front of me. Listening in my darkened bedroom or the crowded school halls, my headphones always on, I'd hummed along.

> I'll kill myself.
> I'd rather die.
> If you could see the future,
> You'd know why.[2]

Now I faced a mutilated body, starvation and contaminated water. Just enough food, now, if I slaved all day for it. Just enough water — and it sure wasn't being boiled to kill the germs. Suppose the eggs were rotten? Suppose the pieces of snake infected the whole soup?

I slumped down hopelessly.

But when the gull returned, I threw four stones so fast that its wing smashed and it sprawled flat. I killed it with a heavy rock, plucked and gutted it, adding it to the pot.

> Getting lost within myself,
> Nothing matters, no-one else;
> I have lost the will to live,
> Simply nothing more to give. . .[3]

No!

I leaped to my feet and raced to the beach. Luckily there was no boat in sight or I'd have stupidly walked right into it. I swam along the shore, pausing to scrub myself with the coarse sand from the sea-bottom. Swimming was easy once you learned to stay with the current and let it do the work.

I scanned the sea for fish, the shore for driftwood. Nothing. But on the way back I swam close to some tall black rocks further out and spotted shells fastened thickly. In that sheltered area the waves were gentler and I could pry with my fingernails. One shell broke loose, so suddenly that all its juice spilled out. But the meat was sweet and delicious.

I hung on the rocks with one hand and got eight more, letting the liquid pour down my throat, eating slowly and sensuously. The others stubbornly resisted every attempt to remove them. So I carefully marked the distance from shore and swam back. I'd need a knife.

The sailor was moaning feebly, restless and in pain. I lathered on all the rest of that tube's ointment and got him to swallow a good bit of stew.

Always watching for boats, never standing against the skyline, I went again for water. There wasn't any other source of water so far. But this, at least, seemed no lower. I kept hoping and searching for a hidden spring beneath the island's surface.

He was awake this time. His eyes were dull; he shivered in the afternoon sunshine. But I felt the fever as I poured water into him.

He lay back with a groan and tried to focus on me.

'Men. . .' he paused, helplessly. 'They come back.'

My heart pumped heavily. 'Now?' I glanced behind us.

He shook his head, opened and closed his hands twice.

'Twenty. . .'

He nodded.

'Hours?' No. 'Days?'

He opened and closed one hand.

'They'll come back in twenty-five days?' He grunted wearily in assent.

'But why?'

'*Los huevos.*' And suddenly was so deeply asleep that he could not be wakened.

I crawled along the rocks, checking, but there was no boat. Surely they didn't suspect anything but an accident?

So they watched. What for? And they would return.

For the eggs.

The whole thing was simply nonsense. They want eggs, so they smash them? They wait almost a month and come back?

Why?

Twenty-five days — almost a month. It sounded like a number I should be familiar with. The length of. . . a menstrual cycle?

I suddenly noticed that no birds were on the beach. And that there had not been any this morning, either.

The sun was scorching hot, but the birds had to be found. The men were still unconscious. I hunted among the sad bits of clothing from the boat's locker and found a workshirt. Heavy though it was, it protected my shoulders from the worst of the sun and it was tough enough to pile eggs in. I took the pail — I never moved anywhere without it now — and a handful of the berries. I set off to find the birds. All we needed was to have them disappear and we'd be done for.

But the birds were there. I came over the rise and

into the valley to discover them poking their sloppy nests back together. The square was being re-formed, just as if nothing had ever happened.

I squatted, watching. They were prey, but I didn't look at them that way. Only that they had to eat and so did we. I would kill them if I had to. But with no joy. None of my father's wild hilarity when he drove home with a dead buck on the fender, all the men smelling of smoke and liquor.

This was more like. . . companionship.

Every so often I changed position because my legs cramped. But I watched and the birds tolerated me, until I came too close.

I went back to gulp the soup, but the men slept on. So I filled the water bucket once again and found some eggs on the hillside. There was a bird that screeched at me, but could not fly. I killed it, messily, and sniffled as I pulled out handfuls of white and black feathers. It went into the pail.

The birds showed no interest in me and suddenly I realised why. They were mating again. By the hundreds and thousands they courted and bred; I watched in wonder and in awe.

They were completely absorbed in their tasks. And I could see them repeating their mistakes: the inexperienced or weaker ones still building on the edge of the square where they were so vulnerable.

The vast loneliness of the island weighed down. The birds seemed the only creatures alive and with purpose. On the wreckage of that ruined square they built again rapidly, blindly, as if there were not a second to spare. The Heermann's gulls guarded everyone and I was pecked severely many times when I located eggs missed by the raiders. Some chicks had survived in spite of everything — and some eggs. Those I marked for another day.

I circled the salt-flats, already noisy with the in-rushing tide, and climbed, surefooted at last, back to camp.

I stayed well below the skyline.

Luckily, because as I peered over the cliff where the fisherman had fallen, there was a blinding glitter. And the red and black boat. Someone on board had field glasses.

With infinite caution I looked not over, but around the largest boulder. The glasses gleamed in the sun and then moved on, sweeping our whole part of the island. Hadn't they found the fisherman's body? Did they suspect we were here?

Why did they watch?

I didn't move until the engines started and the boat chugged softly away. It travelled north as all the boats had on the killing day. Its shadow lay ominous across the water and the muted engine was more frightening than any noisy one could have been.

When I came back, the sailor was lying with his eyes wide open. For a terrible moment I thought he was dead, he was so motionless. But he tried to smile and his colour was a little better. He pointed towards the sea, pantomiming the boat. I showed him how they'd held the glasses on us, moving them back and forth.

He looked worried. *'Se fué?'* and he must have meant had they gone, because when I nodded he relaxed.

'Por qué?' I asked him. 'Why?'

'Los pájaros.'

I was impatient. 'They look at the birds? Why? What do the birds. . . '

'Huevos. Eggs. They want eggs.'

'But why did the man attack me?' I acted out the threatening club. 'He wanted to kill me!'

'No,' his voice was hoarse and trembly, 'just want catch you. Think you tell.'

I fed him, unconvinced. Maybe he was trying to persuade himself. A few spoonfuls of eggs, water, then more eggs until he turned away and would take no more. Then I forced the rest into his brother.

The bird's carcase went in the hot water while I soaked off Juan Jose's bandages. I poured off some of the cooled boiled water from the other pail, sponging him down. He was more restless that afternoon, reaching to touch his brother, who never responded; and to touch his own burned side and his lower back. There was nothing to cushion him from the rocks except the few pieces of clothing.

I had worked the new jeans off him because it was impossible to clean him properly. I wiped him again and again. But so small an amount of fluid passed through him that I began to suspect his back pain was his kidneys, overworked and agonising.

He should have fluids. In a hospital he'd have been hooked up to an IV. The burned parts smelled worse. His mumblings were louder; wild rushes of words spewed out, so fast I couldn't understand a thing. Except that he was talking about the birds, the eggs. . . *way vos mah gee cose.*

I gasped. Magic eggs. That's what he'd been saying. . . that the eggs were magic!

Well, of all the stupid, superstitious nonsense. . . magic eggs, for the love of. . .

Tiredly I sprawled on my flat rock. In this day and age. . . magic eggs.

Not that it mattered. If he thought they were magic and the fishermen thought they were magic, as far as they were concerned, they were magic.

Why the early morning visit, stealthy and secret? Maybe just to get it out of the way before starting a full work day? I could understand now why they might want to steal magic eggs. But to smash them? And why was the boat snooping and scouting out there?

Hastily, I peered over the rocks. Nothing on this side. But then, around the far rocks, came a boat — not the deadly red-and-black. No binoculars. Noisier. He moved quickly away, just a casual late afternoon check.

'*Oye!*'

The scream came from behind me.

The sailor was on his feet, waving and shouting. I whirled in panic. His knees buckled and he fell into my arms. Even with the weight melted off him by the fever, he was a dead weight and we toppled heavily to the ground. He lay there babbling in delirium, while I crept to the rocks and peered between them.

But the ship had gone.

Fright changed to fury and I grabbed him from the good side and hauled him to his knees. 'Get up!' I shrieked. 'Up!'

Dizzily he made it to his feet and we wove our way back to the overhanging ledge. He went down with a groan and his eyes closed. He might have been dead. But when I leaned over there was the faithful heart, still faintly thumping. His flesh was almost sizzled. His breath and burns stank worse than ever, but he *was* alive.

I was not completely alone — not yet.

Covering them with the tarp for shade, I took the pail to the beach. The boat was really gone. I swam, scrubbed with sand and then carried a sharpened rock out to the off-shore boulders. The scallop-things I pried off carefully, saving a lot of their juice, although balancing the full pail was tricky. I left them to cook in the hot water and found half-a-dozen eggs.

When I got back, the salty water was really hot and the scallops jumped and bubbled in it.

Firmly, I lifted the sailor over on his back, ignoring his groans, and pulled open his lips from the side. I poured in eggs and stroked his throat till he swallowed; I switched to his brother and did the same thing.

I was ravenous by then. Mashing the scallops with a flat stone, I fed them both as much as they would take, my mouth watering at the familiar odour. Scallops in garlic butter, slices of thick Italian bread. . . even the red and white tablecloths of that tiny restaurant. . . were clearer, for a moment, than the real face on the rocks.

His eyes opened, blurrily.

'*Huevos magicos,*' I told him in a hushed voice.

'*Magicos,*' he repeated. And fell back.

I put the pail down very, very slowly. He was only asleep. But from his look and the smell of his wounds, he must have aid soon.

I stuck my hand in the bucket and scooped handful after handful of the scallops, gulping them till there was only liquid. Then I up-ended the pail and finished every drop.

The sun dropped into the ocean and the quick dark came.

I moved around with the last of the twilight, checking on the men, relieving myself, my stomach uneasy with the unaccustomed hot food — almost enough, for once.

But with the darkness, the problems came.

There soon would be no eggs left. The ones still here would be chicks any day; the others wouldn't be born for at least three weeks. So the sailors would have no more magic eggs.

Birds were left, plenty of them, but they were probably full of parasites. Bad for sick men. Maybe it would be better to just signal the red and black boat. Get it over with.

I felt like a pinpoint on a vast map. I could see myself from above, through layers and layers of air. Like a doll sitting on a huge rock.

Alone.

But that wasn't true. The doll had other dolls nearby, sick and hurting. And without her help, those other dolls weren't going to make it.

I sighed. Another night to get through. I'd always been a poor sleeper, wakeful and unrelaxed, in that other life. This time I must have tossed and turned for one whole minute before falling into dreamless sleep.

9

Surviving

TWO DAYS PASSED. THREE. The men clung to life.
I filled water pails, washed the men, found eggs and
scallops, watched for the watchers. Twice I dreamed
that rescue ships came, but no-one was on board.
Awake, I knew that even the ship's dinghy had sunk,
or somebody had found and hidden it.

The only thing that changed was the birds. Their
nests were finished and the birds mated nearby.
Heermann's gulls stalked the perimeter, pouncing on
unwary terns and shoving them around. The terns
seldom fought back — just squawked, like people
who want something done. But not by themselves.

It was mesmerising to watch them. If my pad and
charcoal had been there, I'd have sketched them all.
The gulls with their wide red beaks warned me off.
And the terns — two different kinds. One was bigger,
sturdier, and its cry was *kee-e-er*. The other. . . I strained
to imitate its call.

But the sketching pad hadn't come on the trip. My art teacher had been enthusiastic enough to write a glowing note home about my only real skill. Foolish of her. All my art materials had disappeared one day. Into the garbage?

Of course, a sketch pad was easy to get. Even the little stores in La Paz had oils, watercolours, easels. I'd come back some day. Really sit here and watch. Paint them as they flew and mated and died. Study these survivors.

I stopped, puzzled. The idea of even outlasting this place was crazy. Coming back? And yet. . . a decent heavy tent, foam sleeping bag, canned food. It could be done! But that meant the birds would still be here. And how could that be?

If the fishermen came, for whatever insane reason, and broke the eggs each time they were laid, how could the birds survive? How often did they mate?

Surely the birds must fly away before the September rains, otherwise the valleys would be lakes and the chicks would drown. Twenty-five days. I counted back.

So that meant some birds arrived in March and those had chicks. Some in April. You couldn't count on their all coming on the same day, like the swallows of Capistrano on St Joseph's Day. Twenty-five — just about the same as my own cycle. And what would I do about tampons then? Gran had told me once that in the concentration camps of Hitler and Stalin the women's bodies reacted to hunger and stress by just. . . stopping. Some never had another period until they were free.

Free.

But how few had been freed! And the ones who were, like Gran, were those who'd made up their minds to survive. To get back to life, to testify against the murderers. Or, like Corrie Ten Boom, to build a better world. If I were freed. . .

I snapped back to the present. We needed water, eggs if any were left, a bird or two. Freedom would come later.

The taste of fishy eggs, fishy-tasting birds, fishy shell-things was pretty monotonous. But in the spas my mother had gone to, they'd always put her on a diet, made her swim in mineral baths, given her exercises against flab.

I looked down at my stomach and noticed its flat hardness for the first time. My meaty white thighs were dwindling down. And I was tanning all over. The one thing spas never would allow was so much sunlight. No point in being rescued only for cancer surgery. . . I burst out laughing.

The terns flew up, wild with fright. I'd never made a noise here, certainly never laughed before. Rising slowly, I picked my way, finding the few eggs jealously guarded. No wonder — their only chicks.

'My only chick,' my mother's silvery-steel voice floated from the past, 'costs me a fortune in shrinks' fees.' She'd laughed delightedly. 'And diets. . . all dead weight.'

Right, Mother. That dead weight I've been lugging around on my body — and in my head — all these years. What a fool I've been! What a fool! Getting back at you, getting even with *you*, by loading myself with. . . with dead weight.

When I got back to camp, he was gone.

Dropping the pail, I ran back and forth, searching madly. No sign of a boat, no sign of him. I'd caught four birds — we were going to have a feast! He must be here — he must! I collapsed on the ground, panting heavily in the super-heated air.

Pails were there, rags, the tarp, the always-silent brother. Everything in place. Even some scallops that I'd put on a rock to dry were there. Only he was gone.

I hesitated. Should I call? Should I wait there? In the shadow of the rock, the camp and everyone in it were invisible but, as soon as we left, the watchers could see us perfectly.

I peered out cautiously. There was no boat in sight. But it might come around the sea lion rocks at any moment. And they'd see me first, because I had to watch each step on the water-slicked rocks. I started on hands and knees, calling softly.

'Juan Jose! *Oye!*'

I looked behind me again and again for the boat. It was impossible to explain to myself the real terror I felt of the man in it. Intuition? But I'd never had any such feelings before. There was absolutely no reason for it; yet if he came now. . . My legs became quite weak and I nearly lost my balance.

I searched for what seemed like hours, hoping that the men were fishing and wouldn't check until night. Why had I left? Why had I stayed away so long? I'd known he was wild with fever the day before. There was no sign of him.

I began to pray, gabbling promises to God until I heard myself and stopped, appalled. I forced myself to sit and take deep breaths, while my heartbeats slowed.

'O Lord, help me to find him. I'm afraid to be alone.' I paused, ashamed. 'And he's so sick.'

In the silence, I suddenly heard him crying, *'Dios! Dios!'* and knew he was calling on God, too. He sounded very weak.

I called and he cried out once. Then it was silence; even the birds were still. Only the slap of waves.

I located him slumped between two huge rocks. He'd fallen. The bandages were torn away. I ran to the beach, careless of watchers, and drenched him with pail after pail of water. At least the sand and blood washed off. Nothing more to do except give him all the water he could swallow, drop by cautious drop. It seemed to take hours. The sun was unmerciful. In a month or two. . .?

Three times I left him and slid gratefully into the water. It was dangerous. The rocks there were incredibly slick and it would have been easy to jam a foot between them and never get it out. Other spots were dry and sunny — perfect for snakes. So I went warily, like an animal, but I went, because the heat was unbearable. Each time I brought water to sponge him. He shivered and sweated, skin dull with sickness. When he woke up he didn't recognise me, just stared at the unfamiliar place, bewildered.

At last he roused enough for me to get him up, obediently, leaning his full weight on me. How had he ever made it this far?

His legs trembled like an old man's. We stopped often to rest. When we stumbled into camp, I gave a great sigh of relief. We'd seen no ships and now they couldn't see us. The camp was a mess; all the stuff that had fallen from the pail, making the ground slimy. We wove in and out.

He barely made it, past his brother, to the pile of soursmelling clothes. I forced more water into him and smelled a sharp ammonia odour; a stain spread over the ground. It was a hopeful sign: if his kidneys kept working, he had a chance. I'd thinned eggs in the water, but even so he wouldn't eat much.

I left it for a while, then tried again. Each time he took a little before his lips and throat tightened too much to swallow. Finally, he lay back and made snoring noises. I could hear him, as I fed his brother, and it sounded as if there was another difference — a sort of bubbling. Did his lungs have fluid in them? For all I knew, he might be developing pneumonia — and I could do nothing for him here, nothing! What a stupid, useless fool I was! Abruptly, I jumped to my feet and headed for the beach.

Luckily, I'd stooped automatically and, because of

the heat, had moved slowly. Otherwise the man with the binoculars could not have failed to see me. With infinite slowness I sank below the overhanging rocks.

It meant that I couldn't see him either. Just that one glimpse — the red-and-black boat, so very close to our beach, the glasses flashing as he scanned the upper levels, the rocks, the shore. I was afraid he'd come on land, but that was not to be, today, for his ship began to move off with that soft, sinister *chug-chug*.

Risking a glimpse from the side of some low rocks — I had to chip away a few spy-holes — I saw no-one on deck. Maybe he travelled alone, fished alone and spied alone. And the others reported to him. But what did they report about?

It must be that the fishermen would come again to smash more eggs. But the sailor had said 'to steal' the eggs. So they would come ashore. In three weeks. My sailors would not last that long.

The ship disappeared around the cliff where no sea lions played that day. I crouched there, miserable again. What if he had found us? What could he do, really?

The trouble was, I didn't know. We could be taken back as dead bodies. Or traded for something else. Like what? After all, it couldn't be against the law to smash eggs, could it? Even to steal them all, if they wanted to?

But if this were a secret place, a place that no-one knew about, perhaps it had some great value, especially for poor fishermen. The problem went around and around till my brain was weary.

I swam near the shore, ducking back frequently. But then I realised that each lookout couldn't spend his whole day watching. One came in the morning, just as the mist rose, then he or someone else came at sunset. Why had he changed the schedule today? There was absolutely no way to tell. And the sailor, who might have known, couldn't explain.

We had survived. I'd made lucky — or guided? — choices so far. And now there was a life or death decision for all three of us. I'd have to make it, but only God had the answer.

Heads popped up out of the water in front of me, the sea lions playing their games of 'boo!' and 'I see you!' They flopped on their backs and waved their flippers, or held them close to their bodies. It had to be a way of keeping themselves warm or cooling off. They'd ducked out of sight of the boat, but frolicked with me quite unconcerned.

Probably they'd have made a decent meal for us and their fur would be heaven to lie on, but I didn't think I'd be able to look into their eyes and kill them.

And even as the thought came, I knew I would. If I had to and if I could. But they'd never let me get that near — and they were experts in the water. How could any human catch hold of those slippery-smooth bodies?

As the current carried us past their rocks, I squinted from the sun deep into the darkness of the caves. There were shadows in there, shadows I had seen the first day, but which I'd forgotten. An enormous figure seemed to move there in the dim twilight. Not sea lions; much, much bigger. Something gleamed, reflecting the sunlit waters.

And then the waves swept us past and I felt that the sea was no longer warm and buoyant, but icy-cold. The things staring from the gloom were from old nightmares: darkened bedrooms, alley corners on a dusk-filled street. They touched a darkness still inside of me and ready to come out with just a little, little push.

The sea lions were astounded when I thrust with all my strength against the waves and hurled up water all around us. Suddenly, I became an unwelcome visitor and they disappeared instantly. I fell on the beach, exhausted.

10

Alone

LONG FINGERS OF SHADE lay across the camp when I finally returned, carrying water and a few eggs. Juan Jose lay on the ground, still making the snoring noises; his brother was motionless.

I slumped down. This was the worst hour of the day. Even waking up, tight with apprehension, unrested, was nothing to the pit that waited at the day's end. All the work of staying alive, another night to get through, and this time a decision to be made that would save or lose our lives. There was no more time.

For a single moment I felt sympathy for my father with his eagerly awaited cocktail. Just something to hold off the night and all the business still to be done.

Juan Jose's brother had died. His body lay curled and small in death.

For a long time I knelt beside him, unable to feel anything but a vast weariness. Not guilt — he'd never had much chance. Not sorrow — we'd never spoken one word to each other. Emptiness.

Mindlessly, I mixed the eggs and water and fed them to Juan Jose. More than fishy-tasting, almost rotten. I drank the rest, closing off my nose against the smell, swallowing hard to keep them down. He lay with eyes closed, unresponsive to being lifted or lowered. He was still naked, but I was far from reacting; it was like touching a piece of still-warm meat.

I was hungry — terribly, terribly hungry. I was ashamed — a man had died and all I could think of was myself — but I searched the camp for anything at all to eat. The biscuits and dried meat were long gone; the birds from yesterday were a total loss, decayed in the sun where I'd dropped them. The drying scallops were chewy and I finished them off, but they weren't enough.

There were still the sardines. Those were supposed to be saved for the hard times coming, but I didn't care. I wanted them now. I needed them now. Crunchy, very salty. A wonder the birds hadn't found them.

A few of the cherry fruits remained; they lasted a long time, rolled around and around in my mouth. As I swallowed the last of them, I tried to make plans.

First, one man was dead, the other dying. There was no mistaking that sweetish stink, the fever consuming him, the foul smell of his breath.

Second, there was no medicine left. There was nothing on this barren island that could save him. Maybe there were herbs right in front of me, but I'd never know them.

Third — oh, this was so stupid, counting *first, second, third*! A pointless waste of time! I tried to force away the grey film that touched my thoughts, the mists I'd walked through for years. All hopeless. End it all — go out and wait on the beach.

But a tiny, persistent caution warned me to wait. I would not walk blindly into the enemy's territory, like the terns. The fishermen might only have wanted to grab, not kill me. Their leader might have an interest in saving us. Maybe.

Awkwardly, I knelt on the cooling ground. 'Help me. Help. Oh God, please help.'

After a long while I got up and sat on a flat stone, my body complaining of raw scrapes, sunburn, hair caked with salt, stiff and sore. I smelled my own sweat and what I'd eaten coming out of my pores. A real mess.

Maybe — the thought struck from nowhere — I could bring them both down to the beach. They'd be spotted easily. If only it weren't the leader! I shivered uncontrollably just thinking of him. Yet the others must be decent human beings who'd save a sick man. I began to plan excitedly. A dead man. Another who couldn't explain what happened. His wreck of a shirt as a marker. Get them on shore early.

Robbers wouldn't be threatened by an unconscious man, but. . . they'd be threatened by me. If they left him, he'd be no worse off. But his chance — his only chance — was there. They could take him to a town, a doctor, at worst somebody with herbs or something. Even in small towns there'd be burn lotions, wouldn't there? Antibiotics, a telephone?

Yes, they'd save him. But I'd be a danger.

So I couldn't leave. I'd wait in hiding and. . . I might be able to protect him if anyone tried him. I'd stay behind and hope for another chance.

And when they came back to kill the birds, I'd hide. If they hunted me, I'd have sharp stones and those caves might be a good hiding place. No. A sudden reminder of the dark shapes made me pause. There must be better places. I'd search everywhere. The answer had slipped into my mind as if it had been my own solution. But, of course, it wasn't. It had been put there by someone else.

There'd been no idea of surrender. I was realising I had a life to live, after all — a life to protect. I wasn't going to throw it away.

Groping around in the dark, I gathered our few pitiful belongings. The dead brother still lay on the tarp. Slowly I backed down the familiar track to the water, pulling him along. I left him where the tide couldn't reach. It was important that he be buried by his own people.

I hoped Juan Jose knew I'd done my best. Softly, I whispered a prayer for him and left him face down.

The tarpaulin I brought back. There were the pails, the few cloths, the empty medicine chest — I rolled all of it in and tucked the edges closed.

A cool wind blew that night, swirling dust and chilling my bare feet. Thoughts of jobs to do in the morning chased endlessly in my brain. Finally, I curled up with my back to the sailor, getting some warmth from his feverish skin. At some point I fell deeply asleep.

When I woke, it was with a start, panicked for a minute that I had let it go too late. But it was still dark, stars gleaming off the rocks to help me see.

He slept heavily. I shook him, but there was no response and I felt despair. To decide to get him to the beach was one thing; without his help it would be impossible.

I shook him, yelled at him and at last slapped his face. He stirred, heavy with dreams, and called me Rosa. I tried to wrestle him to a sitting position, but he kept falling back, talking fast and slurred so I could understand nothing. Finally, I got him to his feet and dragged his arm around my shoulder.

We staggered down the little incline like a couple of drunks. Weaving and bouncing off the boulders, stumbling in the loose, shifting sand, we made it to the rocky edge of beach. His knees gave way as we reached the highest rock — one where he'd be easily spotted, but safe from the tide. Only I hoped it wouldn't be that long.

It was the usual grey misty morning, wisps of fog

melting near the shore. He lay slack and heavy, heartbeat *thock-thock-thocking* against all odds. When he was arranged, almost like a corpse with his wreck of white shirt flapping a truce, I touched him once. Goodbye. No response.

The delay almost trapped me.

I heard the boat and flung myself towards the pile of rocks. The same ones we'd landed at — how long ago? Years? I looked back over my shoulder to the sea. Oh, thank God, thank God, it wasn't the black-and-red, but another with three or four men on board.

Flat on my stomach, I crawled to our camp. The sound of their excited voices was reassuring. They'd seen one of the sailors, at least. Scrambling to the place where our stuff had been laid, I piled things together. Stealthily, because sound travelled strangely here, I checked again. Nothing left. Back and forth with a branch, wiping dust over the footprints, spilled food and medicine.

Looked all right. *Go!*

It was a wrench that I hadn't expected, leaving it all behind. It was 'our camp' and it meant coming back to find human beings waiting for me, needing me.

Faster. Move faster.

Their boat was grating on shore when I reached my lookout spot, sharp stone in hand. But there was no need. One man was carrying the dead body. Two others were lifting Juan Jose tenderly. Thank

God, he'd get help in time.

I relaxed. In the bright sunshine the doubts of last night seemed ridiculous. Why not go down, ask for help, maybe offer them money? I hesitated, started to rise.

It was then that the leader's boat joined them. I shrank back.

Shouts and commands from his boat sent men up the hill towards me. The nearest was his second-in-command, a man with a dark angry face. His eyes flickered from the path to the birds to the surrounding rocks. He never took his right hand out of his pocket.

I remained motionless. The others turned back, but this one scanned the area with suspicion. He yelled a string of words — curses? — down to the boats. And then he was called back. He went, but reluctantly, continuing to look behind him as if he were not satisfied. Somewhere I'd heard that certain animals sense that you're staring at them. I forced myself to look away from him. After a thousand years he joined the others. The motors started up. They were leaving the island and I would be alone.

Completely alone.

As the throb of engines died away, the silence surged back. Not complete silence. The lap of waves against the shore was clear, the whiny little breeze that only came in the mornings. And the birds. Always the birds. And above all, a kind of. . . presence.

Leaning against a boulder, I took a deep, relieved breath. The tension washed out of me. No big rush to get food or medicine or water. No-one to worry about. From the minute the boat had exploded, I'd been moving without a chance of rest or thought. Now there was all the time in the world. I dozed comfortably. . . Juan Jose had his medical care. . . I had my clothes to wash. . . My new camp should be closer to the spring . . . I'd missed a swim this morning. . . I drifted. . . half awake.

One by one the sounds quietened, until there was absolute silence. The light strengthened, becoming luminous, shimmery. Instantly wide-awake, heart fluttering, I scrambled awkwardly to my knees, scraping them bloody on the rocks.

Nothing.

Yet someone was near, very near.

Every sense sharpened. I felt the puckered burn of my ear, the sore rough flesh of elbows and feet. My whole left side throbbed. Aching eyes, always gritty from the whirling sands, began tearing and I scrubbed at them with calloused fingers.

A figure came towards me into the light. Or maybe it *was* the light. And as it moved closer, all the fear and pain dropped away, like stones being pulled from the beach out into the endless sea. There was no time — just the gentle light surrounding me. And him.

But I was grateful, so grateful, to be on my knees, because that was where I belonged. Shame filled me as I felt his presence and remembered what my life had been. Not sins of sex — but only because my unattractiveness had repelled everyone. Nor drugs. No, what I thought of were the times I could have opened up — to my mother, my dad. Instead, I'd curled myself into a hate-filled balloon, as prickly to touch as the cardamon cactus around me now.

No tears came. Only a rusty whisper, 'Oh God, I am so sorry. . . so sorry. . .'

How long did I kneel there? I'll never know.

The light departed and sound returned. I looked up, bewildered, to see only rock and sand. All the pain was gone; for the first time since the explosion I drew in a full breath without an ache in my ribs. Peace blew through me like the whirlwind, scattering my past, gradually filling me to the brim.

I stood erect and flung my arms to the brazen sky. There was no enemy, no-one at all in sight. Only now could I see the incredible beauty of this island that had seemed so stark and barren.

Then, suddenly, everything was as it had been before. Well, no. Never the same, never that.

I bent down and picked up my life again and behold, it was all brand-new!

Back to the spring. Dumped the clothes that reeked of sickness. I drank and drank and drank. Searching carefully, I discovered a place where the hill had split — a nice little hiding hole for me. One pail I left by the spring, the other two came along as a permanent part of me. I never let myself be silhouetted against the skyline. Someone might be watching — an uncomfortable thought.

Just the same, I swung the pails cheerfully. The swishing sound was pleasant. So was the sun, not broiling hot out here where the breezes blew fresh. The weather was perfect — a day very much like the one when the boat sank.

I allowed myself to think of the crew, my parents, lying fathoms deep under the ship or moving gently through the currents of the sea. Probably not much left of them now. All their pain gone. All their wantings. My mother's craving for every juicy bite of life. . .

She and my father seemed like persons I'd read about long, long ago.

At last I said goodbye to them. Two people who'd just happened to have me. A concession, my dad admitted often enough, to the son he so desperately wanted. And then to get stuck with *me*! Not their fault. Not mine.

I couldn't wish myself back into that life, ever. Living in the same space, but always kept at arm's length. Never able to measure up — except with Gran. The times I'd spent with her while Dad was drying out in one fancy sanatorium after another — those were memories of love, the only ones I'd ever known. My mother had dropped me there with relief and collected me with a sigh.

But I was a different Jen now — alive, sunburned, weight dropping rapidly. I should have been worried about losing it so fast, about vitamins, the tiny water supply, instead of whistling. But my bare feet had toughened; burning rocks no longer bothered me. I was going to find some fish, a bird or two, more berries. And go swimming.

I slid in like a seal, light-hearted. Float. . . swim. . . float. . .

Finally I crawled out, waterlogged, and lay concealed from view. Maybe one day there would be a pleasure boat going past, like the one we'd been on. Those would be the ones to signal. Exactly how, I couldn't imagine.

I brought out the dirty clothes. The blouse and underwear were rags. Salt embedded in the seams had worn the fabric paper-thin. The jeans were barely shorts. Even the sailor's tough leather belt was weakening, but it was the most necessary part. It chafed my hipbones uncomfortably, but it held up what was left of the jeans. And my sharp little stone dagger.

After they'd been gingerly washed and spread on the hot stones, I slipped naked into the sea.

The scallops came off smoothly under the edge of my knife. I spilled no more than a drop of juice and chewed each mouthful luxuriously. There were more of them and easier to find. I watched carefully for lookouts, for I was vulnerable in the water. The boats could be behind any rock and spot me long before I saw them. And my hair was growing too fast; the chopped-off strands blew around my face. Constant sunlight had turned it to a streaky gold, making me far too visible against the dark blue water.

I dog-paddled back to my clothes. They were still damp. Chilled by the long swim, I stretched out flat and drifted off again.

The drone of an engine entered my dream. It was a dream, I knew that — the rocks under me were rough and hot. Waves were slap-slapping against. . . against a boat.

We were in the small boat, going to look for whales. Juan Jose was repairing the motor which kept stalling. We sweated in the sun while he cleaned off the salt, wiping his hands on his pants. Both keys in place, quarter turn right, and they were on. Throttle in neutral. Ready. Panic rose in my throat as he reached for the switch.

Before my scream ripped out, he turned to me with a very superior frown. 'No danger, *señorita*.' Why, he'd spoken perfect English all the time and only pretended not to understand me! 'On the ship the helping generator was petrol-powered and some fuel must have leaked into the bilge. When Esteban tried to start, a spark blew us apart. This is different.'

One motor caught very quickly, very loudly; the other ground noisily for several seconds. The sailor was talking over the racket, but he was talking Spanish again. Why? Now I'd insist he speak English to me. . . The Spanish grew louder, quicker, and I woke. And lay absolutely still.

The voices were real and very near.

It took every ounce of willpower to stay motionless. One arm was asleep and I dared not move it. A light flickered on rock directly above me and I tensed, ready to run — where?

But it must have only reflected off his binoculars, because it passed on. And so, after a while, did the boat. But it seemed a very long while and I was sweating, chilled, pins and needles all over when at last I dared to move.

They were still watching, but not ready to come ashore.

Yet.

God, oh God, don't leave me all alone and forsaken!

11

Cramp

AS MY HEARTBEAT SLOWED, I gathered the dried clothing and pulled it on. Then I scuttled along behind the protecting rocks until there was a decent view.

Nothing at all was in sight.

Right then, hungry as I was, I started to chip away at the rocks. It was impossible. So I moved along until I found a kind of natural hole. My pointed dagger widened it enough to see one view. There were a few other spots, but making peepholes ruined my knife; the bigger the hole, the more damage the knife took. I rubbed sand in the cut places to make the holes look natural.

The sun was near the horizon when I reached the spring. I drank deeply, the blunted stone so near my hand that, when a yellow-legged gull got too close, I broke its wing. Another rock slowed it even more; I finished it off.

The insides were still warm and there were two yellow balls inside it. Not diseased; these were un-hatched eggs. I swallowed them whole. They tasted like the eggs from home — no shell, just yolk and not so fishy.

The gutted body was hung in the shade while I hunted for others. Four I caught by surprise, together in a little bunch of loose twigs; I swung the bucket wildly and only one got away. I ate all their eggs. They didn't fill me, but at least the meatiest parts could be cut up in salt water tonight to make a kind of stew for tomorrow.

I fell asleep with a fuller stomach, but with uneasy twinges of guilt about the birds. They trusted me a little and I'd taken advantage of them. But what else was there for me to do? I'd seen no more snakes, no berries. The scallops were all right, but I needed something more substantial.

I lay snugly in the pile of clean rags. There were a million stars and I tried to recognise them, drowsily reminding myself to find sardines, switch the birds to a pail of fresh water, locate spyholes. . .

No dreams, no worries about the sailors. After midnight, a delicious coolness made me burrow deeper into the pile of clothing.

When I woke up, the sun had risen. From here the entire island was visible, but no-one could see me. I stretched. All my muscles felt looser, springier. I wrapped my arms around my knees. I could do some spying myself. No need to sneak into the water — it would be a longer walk for a swim, but I didn't tire as much as I used to in spite of my hunger.

The white square of birds formed and re-formed, the birds swooping over the waves for food, circling back to rag-tag nests. Not the greatest of housekeepers, but better mothers than some humans. Better than. . . no, she'd given me what she was able to give.

Later, when there was time, I'd try to sort out my mother's problems — and mine. For now, it was enough that, waking up today, I was a different person, relaxed and ready for whatever was on the way. I tingled with anticipation — to outwit the killers of birds. And with thankfulness — deep, overwhelming thankfulness to the God who had granted me this gift. That mighty power in the wilderness.

I checked for boats, sea lions, birds. None, none and tens of thousands.

The carcases of yesterday's birds were stiff, but not smelly. I broke them into as many parts as possible. They were oily and the grease felt good on my roughened skin. The bird parts went into the pail of fresh water.

As I went down to the stony little beach, I looked at the birds. They pushed and jostled for good places in the centre, like kids at a rock concert.

Both kinds of terns were scared of the gulls and stayed out of their way. The gulls were afraid of nobody, including me. They screeched when I came too close and lunged at my eyes. They wouldn't be able to do that to the men, though. Their gallantry would have no effect against clubs.

I sat on a rock, imitating the birds' constant wariness, watching the sea and shore as instinctively as they did. The sorrow I felt for the birds, the pity, was out of all proportion. They were birds, only birds. Doomed to extinction as a species, if the men returned to kill or steal.

Could I do anything, anything at all?

I swam and pried off scallops with my newest sharpened little rock, sucking the juices and chewing with real enjoyment. They were no different from an elegant restaurant's oysters on the half shell, but plumper and spicier direct from the sea. I ate and swam, ate and swam from rock to rock.

The glorious sensation of being full again after such a long while made me careless.

So when the pain hit me, I doubled up and went right under. I'd never felt such agony in all my life.

I sank like a stone, unable for several seconds to guess what had attacked me. I could not straighten up. The pain was too awful. My arms still worked, though, and I beat my way to the surface. As my head lifted out of the water, I gave a single shriek. It wasted my only chance to gulp some air.

For a few seconds I lost all sense and struck out in blind panic, smashing madly at the waves. The twisting, grinding torture was so terrible that I went down again, searching fearfully for the shark that must be crushing my leg. But the emerald waters were completely empty. Bewildered, I looked down to see my leg bent sharply at the knee, the foot curled, calf muscles bulging.

Cramp! I burst to the surface.

Not straight up — I couldn't go straight, favouring my right leg with its tendons knotted into wires hard as steel. The shoreline seemed miles away, although I'd tried to stay in close, and the wrenching pain grew steadily worse.

Even then I glanced once, fearfully, over my shoulder. Anyone could have come on me, there, and finished me with one blow. No chance to escape; just like the birds. But there was no-one. Only the empty sea.

I turned again towards the shore. The idea of sinking gently through the water was no longer attractive. That had seemed quiet, painless. This was one red and orange ball of torture creeping up along my right side. If it reached my stomach, it would force my head down into the water and I would not be able to raise myself.

My right arm did not seem to work very well, but I beat and pushed against the waves with both hands, pumping hard with my good leg. How far to shore? Can't be done. Could I grab a rock? There were some: an unexpected swirl of current swept me past before I could grasp them. The next one had green slime that my fingers slipped off. No good.

Abandoning the rocks, I began to slap away at the water like a beginning swimmer, just trying to push myself forward. But the pain, like a tightening vice, blotted out all thought, all will. To have it stop, to have it stop for only a minute . . . I'd do anything.

I went under once more, pulled out and went under again. I was open-mouthed from the spasms and again I swallowed the sea. Heavy with water when I came up, my arms flailed uselessly; the shore was too far.

I closed my mouth the next time, but spun, helpless, away from the shore. Round and round like a top, down, deeper. Deeper. In the depths, 'even there shall your hand hold me. . .'

A touch.

Something in the depths touched me. On the side. On my hand. When whatever it was grazed the bad leg, a pang of anguish shocked me to my senses and forced me to the surface in the greatest terror I had ever known.

The dead sailor. . . sharks. . . barracuda. . . pieces of me falling to the ocean floor. . . I pumped and thrashed to the surface, felt myself pushed from below, struggled forward. . . and bumped into rocks. Shore rocks.

Blinded with pain I fell, crawling onto the beach towards the concealment of the high rocks. With the last of my strength, I looked behind me.

The faces of the sea lions bounced up and down, staring towards me. Silent and intent, only their whiskers twitched. I raised my hand in a half-salute and they vanished.

I slumped down, making a tremendous effort to relax the bunched muscles, hard as iron. My foot was bent inwards and could not be straightened. Pressing the knuckles of my hand on the ugly lumps, I began to probe the hard ball of muscle. Immediately the pain worsened, but I kept it up, clenching my teeth, and at last the tension eased.

Tendons quivered as the leg straightened out. Slowly I moved the pressure down towards the foot and felt the arch muscles loosen. The foot went slack.

Pain and terror receded. I lay flat and cried. At first I only snuffled but, as the tide waters rushed noisily in, I screamed away the fright and hurt of years. My throat was hoarse with salt and yelling when I finally stopped. The hot noon sun was directly overhead, so I crept into a shady hole, blowing my nose into my fingers. I felt headachy and swollen-eyed. But even as I drowsed off I congratulated myself on keeping down the breakfast so dearly paid for. The faces of the sea lions had been familiar, like teachers concerned for my safety. Or hidden, guarding angels?

It was late afternoon when the long cool shadows woke me. I yawned and stretched under the big cardamon cactus. My foot looked perfectly normal.

There was no sign of boats or lookouts. Keeping under cover, I tried walking. My leg seemed weak and I limped, but after a few steps it was fine.

Stopping to view the great white square of birds enlarging itself, I snaked my way uphill. In just this short time they had become familiar friends.

How long had I been here, anyhow?

Counting back, it seemed the days had begun to blur. Why hadn't I cut marks to tell the time? The explosion had been the first week of April, one night in the boat, then the nights on shore — how many? That was so terribly important because only that way could I guess when the men would come back. If the birds left, I couldn't exist. My chance to escape would be when the men returned.

The sun glinted like a beacon from my new camp. I stopped, appalled. Beams of light reflecting off something shiny — it could be seen for miles!

I raced up the hill. This was the time a lookout boat usually came past. I arrived panting, a stitch in my side, but knowing that a couple of weeks ago I could not have run a tenth of the distance.

It was the tin pail. Out in the sun all day, boiling hot to the touch, a bubbling stew of bird parts — and a betraying finger pointing to my exact whereabouts! And I'd put it there myself! I almost flung it down the hill. What an idiot! What a fool! Right back to the same old dumb mistakes.

A look around the horizon calmed me somewhat. Perhaps this evening no-one had come yet; sometimes they stayed late.

Relaxed, I sampled the contents of the bucket and was surprised at the rich brothy taste. The meat had melted off the bones and the scum of beaks and feathers was just skimmed out by my fingers. The pail was too heavy to lift. I stuck my head into it — sucked and gobbled and spat out bones and gristle. About six huge mouthfuls had been gulped when I realised there'd been eyes and things besides meat in there. It didn't bother me a bit.

Towards the last of the soup I forced myself to slow down, to leave some for the morning. But then it might go bad overnight in this heat. Better not take a chance. I finished it off.

The temptation to lick the pail made me tremble from head to foot. But I resisted. I'd remembered Ivan Denisovich who never, ever, licked his bowl. That was the sign of a 'goner' in the Gulag, to lick your bowl. I had finally decided that I did not belong in the company of goners.

Waiting for the rich meal to settle, I scanned the horizon. Nothing. A small uneasiness began. If they'd come earlier, the glinting pail might have been noticed. Just because they weren't here now didn't mean a thing — they might have reported to the leader about a shining where no shining should be. Maybe tonight the ship would come back.

It was a matter of minutes to collect the clothes, the pails, the empty medicine chest. Another camp to find before it got completely dark.

I was fuming. Bad enough to be hungry, to be sunburned, to get a cramp. Being hounded from place to place was too much.

My drinking water was lukewarm, a little brackish as if salt were seeping in. To make it easier, I drank almost all of it and poured the rest over my hair — no need to carry it. Finding a new camp wasn't so hard. No birds came to that spot at all. Safer that way. Birds whirling up at my approach would give away the hiding place. I checked again before setting out for water.

Just as well.

They were going home — three boats, lower in the water than usual. The red-and-black was in front — showing who was leader, making them all follow him, using the glasses. I stayed well hidden, not moving an inch. The tin pail was safely in the shadows. They were careless that night, impatient to bring in the big catch. A quick scan, then on their way. Didn't even shut down the motors.

I filled the water pails and drank thirstily. The soup had been salty and I'd swallowed a good part of the ocean when the cramp hit. Salt was necessary; without it I'd be too weak to move fast when the time was right.

The memory of my near-drowning crossed my mind — sharp and clear but without the terror. No reason to start blaming myself in the old familiar way. Cramps happened. But I promised that I'd never let myself get that far from shore again.

On the way back, I sat down to watch the birds. It was the most fascinating scene in the world. Gulls and terns floated in from the ocean, then out again.

They could have been set to music, with the sea as background, its rhythm louder as the night drew on. A different music altogether from the songs of dying that I'd loved in the past. This music sang of life.

There were pitifully few chicks. When a Heermann's gull started for one unwary tern, I lofted a handful of pebbles at him. They stopped him in his tracks, but he eyed the tern mother as if marking her out for another day. She was pretty dopey, building her nest so close to his edge of the square, not keeping watch for him.

Even if the gull attacked, she could have fought him. They weren't all that different in size. Yet the terns didn't seem to be much for defending themselves: perfect pacifists, many of their chicks maimed or dead.

I knew there wasn't a thing to be done about gulls killing terns. That was nature, admit it. But could I beat the bird-killers? Dusky dark came and still I sat, engrossed in planning a future for the first time in my life. There was an inkling of some tremendous plan. . . for me. . . something to do with the birds, and Gran, and myself. . . to save us all. I slipped down onto my knees.

'I'm still here. On this island where you put me. I didn't die today. You saved me, for some reason. Help me to understand.'

There was only silence. Night wind, wavelets breaking.

No answer.

No answer? But the answers were coming faster and faster into my mind, like data into a computer. Process.

12

Foreboding

PUT THINGS IN ORDER.

Gran. I'd find her, see if we could begin a life together. There must be money somewhere — my father was always complaining about the tons of insurance he had to carry. But if Gran lived with me, I'd have to be responsible. Have to cut a way out of the tough shell I'd built around myself. Could I do that?

On my own? There was God, no question in my mind about that. I knew it as surely as I lived. Each day I'd grown more aware of a presence here. But I knew nothing at all about him. How would I find out?

The birds. There had to be schools somewhere that taught things I really needed to know. Hard things. Ways to save the terns and the gulls. Mean, hard subjects that I'd always avoided — science, physiology, ornithology.

And organisations — where would I find environmental groups that tried to save our world —

especially places like. . . *Pájaros*, had he called it?

I racked my brain to recall any names. Audubon Society. Nature Conservancy. Sierra Club. What others? Any others? Maybe they organised. . . well, travel-study groups for students. Only. . . I didn't want to be part of any Mickey Mouse bunch. This wasn't going to be a one-time fun-time, but a lifetime.

First, of course, there was the small matter of getting away from here, so I could come back. Psychology, flying small planes, chemistry, biology of birds. . .

Drowsy and yawning, I picked up my pails, headed back to the camp. In the pile of clothing I curled up, content.

Then half-rose. Forgot to get a string of kelp. And sharpen another rock. And maybe twist those bird tendons into a slingshot instead of into soup. Well, there were other days. I lay down again. Wonder if bird biology would be a tough course. . .

The days passed quickly, too quickly. Dozens of things had to be done each day just to stay alive, some taking longer than others. It seemed hours to get the fresh water to drip into my bucket; the spring was drying up. And that thought had to be pushed away. Because, without water, there really was no chance at all.

Each morning I travelled across ground that I knew by heart searching for a new spring, with no success. It never rained.

I hunted the birds, but they had become wary.

Sometimes a half day would be wasted before I caught even one. I needed their eggs, their meat and, most of all, their fat. Smeared on my hands and feet, it soothed the cracked and peeling skin.

The only escape from the battering, brutal sun was to swim and gulp sea water. With swallows of salt, I felt less exhausted.

Parts of the birds could be experimented with — tendons, for one thing, to make fishing line or a slingshot. I made one and killed three birds with it. But I didn't keep it moistened, so the thing got brittle and ruined a perfect shot. That was a hungry day.

The kelp lay very deep on the sea bottom, so deep that I came up dizzy and sick from a dive. It was thick with salt, chewy and disgusting. I ate what I could, figuring it must be nutritious.

One fantastically lucky day the birds rose in swarms and flung themselves into the ocean. I raced after them and filled both buckets again and again with sardines. Millions of them in the waves! If I hadn't needed to be on the lookout for the boats, there would have been a year's supply.

As I put them out to dry, all kinds of plans continued to swirl through my brain. Very soon the men would be back and I had to be ready.

Why couldn't I just swim out and wait when I saw them coming? Pretend I'd just fallen overboard that day? I'd be no threat to them. If I reached them before they hit the island, they surely wouldn't have any reason to fear me. I could offer them a reward for calling the police. Except maybe they'd be afraid of the police. Could I steal a boat while they were on the island, start it and escape? But they knew this whole area and I didn't. I made and discarded dozens of plans. And the days were passing, passing, and the men would come soon.

The sardines didn't last. The birds stole them as fast as they were hung out to dry. But if they were left in the pail, they just went bad. So I forced them down, even the ones in the bottom that stank.

Was it the discomfort of those almost-rancid fish that brought on the nightmare? Or something else?

Because she came — Gran — directly towards where I was sleeping in the heat of the afternoon, looking fearfully over her shoulder in the direction of the sea. Her lips moving, she strained to tell me something. But I could not, could *not* make out the words. Danger. I saw that in her face. A warning.

I shot straight up, out of the dream — so real! — onto my hands and knees. The sardines, I tried to tell myself. Yet in all this time, I'd never eaten anything that didn't stay down or that sickened me.

I spun around wildly.

No-one.

It wasn't any kind of physical pain, but a terrible apprehension so that my bladder was too full and I began to gasp for air. Air that I couldn't pull in deep enough. My heart hammered against my ribs till it seemed they might crack.

Yet there was no reason, no reason.

Cautiously I scanned the entire island from my perfect lookout. Still nothing. Warily I crept down the hill and, taking cover behind every rock, slid into the water.

Avoiding the open spaces, I kept the biggest boulders between me and the outer waters where the ships came. It was too dangerous for the fishing boats to come in this close to the rocky shore.

I told myself it was perfectly safe.

But small nerves in my back were jumping. I wore the usual ragged shirt and the jeans that were barely shorts, yet the ocean seemed much colder than yesterday. The uneasiness grew. Maybe I'd caught some deadly sickness from the birds.

I felt weak — and curiously, ravenous with hunger. There was nothing to eat back at the camp, but there were always a few scallops on these rocks. If I hadn't needed those scallops so badly, I'd have gone back to the beach.

And he'd have got me there.

13

A last awful shriek

THERE WERE NO SCALLOPS on this side of the beach. So I drifted with the current, always watching the sea. The dark caves were near, dangerously near, but there were signs that there had been shells attached to these rocks. I swam closer. Deep scratch marks and bits of broken shell showed where the scallops had been clawed off. The marks were deep — and fresh.

The cuts stood out clearly on the green and slimy stones, far too high for me to reach. And I had never dared venture this way before; only hunger drove me now.

I swam from rock to rock; the ugly tears had ripped right through the tiny green moulds that clung so tightly to the boulders. Shreds of growth hung down like emerald icicles. Something had torn the shells loose, something enormously big and powerful.

The dark caves were directly behind me when I

saw the last scallop. Crumbs of shell broke off as I stared, horrified. Liquid was still trickling down, drying as it moved. Whatever had been here was only minutes ahead of me.

I whirled around, obeying too late all the warnings my body had been signalling ever since I woke.

'Hi, there!'

For a second it seemed as if my heart really stopped. Then it began, double-timed, rising up to fill my throat so that I almost choked.

I reached out to cling to the rock, but my hand slid off its slickness.

There was no-one in sight.

No sound of a boat.

'Hey, I know you're there!' His jeering laugh boomed back and forth, bouncing off the rocks in the little cove.

It was the leader, the blond American.

I sank so that only my nose was above water and hung there, motionless.

The shadow came around the rocks first — the huge shadow of a sail. He'd judged the currents and the wind and moved in on me soundlessly.

He was in the dinghy, the one I'd seen aboard his ship that very first day. Only he'd been too smart to use a noisy outboard or even oars. He'd attached a sail. In a moment he was between me and the shore.

He was a superb sailor, manoeuvering the boat in narrower and narrower circles, avoiding the jutting rocks and swinging always between me and the land.

I flinched back against the slippery rock, the sea behind me, the dark caves in front. No escape, no escape, my brain unable to focus on anything except the looming shape above me, the man's wide, white grin. . .

He drove the boat like a heavy battering ram, directly at me. I heard his yell of delight as I flung myself out of his way. Too late I realised I'd lost the small protection of the rock and turned back, desperate to slide under the boat.

He twirled the little craft expertly, so that I came up just where he wanted me.

His right hand snaked out and grabbed a handful of my hair. I shrieked in agony and clawed at his fingers as he dragged me aboard, still grinning. For a minute he held me at arm's length, then simply let go and I fell, moaning, into the bottom of the boat. His smile broadened as he looked down on me, sprawled there at his feet.

He slid the small anchor overboard and quite casually slammed the back of his fist against my jaw. A burning fireball exploded across my head and golden sparks blurred all vision. The pain wasn't enough to stun me, though — it was more like a searing electric shock.

I rolled over the side without thought. Right overboard and came up swimming — for my life.

Towards the caves.

On the sea, in the boat, he had me. Ahead, in the dark. . . maybe. . .

But I heard him howling with raucous laughter, amused at my hopeless attempt to change the odds. 'There's no way out of those caves! No way! C'mon back!' The jeering laugh echoed again back and forth across the rocks. It spurred me to frantic effort — if I could reach the shore ahead of him. . .

And then came the sharp crack of his body hitting the water in a long, shallow dive. All hope washed out of me. He was bigger, stronger; this was his territory: like the Heermann's gulls.

I'd scorned the tame surrender of the terns; was I going to imitate them and give in without a fight? I forced strength into arms that felt boneless; I would not, would not turn to see how close he was behind me. I strained every bit of flesh and muscle. Terror of him, of what he'd do, gave me the power for a fraction of a moment to draw ahead of him.

I judged the waves just a breath quicker, clenched the slick rock seconds before he did. From someone, suddenly, came incredible strength.

Had he seized my ankle, I'd have been in the water and it would have been all over. But he was in no hurry. I heaved myself up on the punishing rocks, rolled awkwardly on my left shoulder and scrabbled into the lightless cave. One second too late his hand clutched the stone I'd just balanced on, and his booming laugh followed me.

The outer passage narrowed to a pair of low tunnels; warm, still air touched my face. He was right: there was no way out or there would have been a breeze, a chink of light.

On torn hands and knees I scrambled deep into the gloom; after the blazing sunlight it was like midnight. A smell filled the place: powerful, animal, stinking. I panicked at the two entrances — which one, which?

Even with the demon behind me, the stench and dimness of the bigger hole terrified me. In the murk something glimmered wickedly, like the eyes I'd seen. I thought I'd seen them again. Stupid with fear, I threw myself into the smaller tunnel. It was barely a scrape in the wall; less than a metre in, my forehead smashed into stone.

The end of the tunnel.

Sobbing, mad with terror, I whirled to face my tormentor. Clutching at the floor, the walls, I searched for a stick, a rock, a shell — anything to fight with. The floor was smooth, wet and empty.

But from the low roof hung icicle-like rocks, sharp as daggers. I filled both hands.

He blocked out the sun as his bulk filled the entrance, moving slowly, sensuously, nearer, picking his way into the dark. 'I'm coming to get you,' he crooned in the long-ago children's game. 'I'm coming . . . to. . . get you. . .'

I flattened myself against the damp cool wall.

'God, God, God.' Only my lips moved. Hopeless, I stifled my gasps and listened to him coming, inexorably, closer. 'Save me, Lord God!'

'Phew!' He'd caught the stinking odour of the

bigger cave. Then he chuckled. Genuine, apprecia-
tive enjoyment. Pitiless.

'So this is where you holed up? I *knew* I'd have a
better chance, trailing you alone! No wonder I never
put the glasses on you! Pretty cute. . . just like
yourself. . . gotcha!' He bellowed with laughter. I
could hear the rasp of cloth against stone as he
crawled into the bigger cave.

'Come out, come out, wherever you are! We'll
have some fun. . .' his voice dropped to hoarse,
insinuating mumbles then rose again, menacing. . .
'I'm warning you. . . come out or else I'll. . . I. . .
a-a-agh!'

He screamed once, piercingly.

The echoes beat against the walls; he screamed
again and again. It was deafening in the small
chamber. There was the sound of something hitting
the low ceiling — a dull thud, as if he'd jumped up
and his head had struck the roof. Snorting and
grunting noises, heavy bodies thumping against the
thin bit of rock that separated the tunnels — and all
in the warm and smelly twilight. Then his last, awful
shriek.

The sounds, the echoes were so magnified that it
was impossible to tell what was happening. Suddenly his whimpering, begging cries began as he tried to
crawl out. He was pleading to be allowed to reach
the entrance. Some heavy thing followed him.

I looked at the gleaming, sunlit water only a few
yards away. And as I stared longingly, he dragged

himself towards it, turning an agonised face to see what followed behind him.

Something blotted out the light between us; a thing so enormous that it seemed to fill the whole cave. Red specks flashed behind my eyes and there was suddenly no air. No way to get enough breath into my lungs. Everything turned misty and dim. Dark. Dark. Nothing.

It could have been only minutes that I blacked out, because the splash, then another, sounded distinctly as two bodies hit the water. I trembled — scraped, naked and sore. At some unknown moment, my bladder had let go and I now sat in a pool of urine. But *he* was gone. I drew some deep shaky breaths. Gradually the shivering began to ease.

It was then I heard the movements. Like a body twisting for a more comfortable position in cramped quarters. Soft, stealthy, fussy little noises. Breathy grunts.

Where? Where?

Surely not — oh, God — not coming back into the cave? I strained to hear, to see. The man had run, but *something* had followed him. The tunnel entrance was empty, touched with golden sunlight.

These sounds were near, very near. They came from inside this same cave.

'Oh, God!' Pure prayer.

Again the brushing sounds. . . something moved just beyond the other side of my wall.

Flesh tore open along my whole right side as I slid and scrambled erect. My upraised hand struck numbingly on the low ceiling and saved me from a concussion. Bent double, I forced myself towards the entrance. *He* waited. And if I escaped, the other — whatever it was — waited, too.

To get out of darkness, not to die in shadows, was my only thought. The lightless waters had seemed so attractive a thousand years ago. Now I just wanted to die in the sunshine.

I plunged forward. The sounds halted abruptly. Stumbling, falling twice, I could feel the blood pouring down my legs. Mad with terror, I somehow reached the mouth of the cave — and pulled up short. I couldn't go forward or back. I gripped the narrow sides of the entrance, frozen. Something behind me. . . something in front. . .

There was nothing. Nothing?

The little cove lay in silence. No birds, no people, nothing. The sun glittered on the sea and on his boat, still bobbing at anchor. The most peaceful scene imaginable.

I crawled over the rocks and lowered myself without a ripple. Salt water bit achingly into my side, setting it on fire. The deep scratches stung. Pain was welcome, otherwise I'd have thought it all a dream. But this was real — must be real! I sank and swam underwater, coming up by the rocks where I'd been trapped. They fell in shadows across me. The water felt like ice and I sensed the deadly,

deadly cold of shock numbing my body.

I clung there, shivering and sick. No sound, no movement, but they were waiting for me, had to be waiting, licking their lips. All they wanted was for me to make a move and then they had me.

It seemed like hours that I huddled there. I felt myself chilling to death, heartbeat slowing, even a little drowsy. A wave slapped over me, filling my mouth with salt and bringing my head up with a snap. I had very little energy left. But I had not come all this way to sink forever in the sea.

I struck out towards the little dinghy and reached it in a few strokes. It was empty. But getting on board was almost impossible, my fingers were so numb. At last I made a final, weak jump and grabbed the seat, hauling myself over the side. I remembered a girl who had nearly capsized a boat like this, who'd wept when she could not get her bulk over the edge.

I fell into the bottom.

The sun was lower now and offered no warmth to my chilled body. I forced myself to shaky knees. The empty boat floated in an empty cove; the sail flapped gently as the afternoon breeze strengthened.

This was a bigger boat than the one from the yacht. I opened the small compartments, searching for a weapon, and found surprising wealth. Liquor, cameras, a pair of German binoculars, a razor-sharp hunting knife — I snatched it.

At the slightest sound I leaped, glaring around me,

expecting his hand to come, any minute, over the side.

Clothes! I snatched at T-shirts, heavy thick pants and woollen socks. Even with them on, the trembling continued. Never taking my eyes off the water or the land for more than a second, I opened a bottle of rum and took two long swallows.

The long shudders slowed down and stopped. I caught myself arguing for a third shot and firmly put the bottle away. I floated, toes and fingers warm at last, clutching the knife in a death-grip. I opened other compartments, all the while watching the water, the cave. Nothing, not even a ripple.

Curious, I examined the boat: small but compact, oars as well as sails, many cabinets. I yanked them open. There were dozens of weapons: knives mostly, but an automatic pistol, too; packages of dried biscuits, cans of meat *with a can opener!* My mouth filled with saliva so fast I began to drool.

14

A step forward

WHEN I LOOKED UP I saw them both.

He floated, slack, the waves pushing him from behind the very rocks where I'd hidden. He looked much smaller, a shrunken little toy-man. There was no blood, but his shirt was gone and he had a tremendous hole in the front of his head.

The other paddled near him, unblinking eyes watching me; a huge, fat and ugly body, covered with greyish-brown fur. Instead of the flat, comic seal face, there was an enormous tube from its eyes to below its chin. It looked exactly like the trunk of an elephant.

An elephant seal.

There were a few in the Sea of Cortez, although the captain had told us that the Baja coast held more. Maybe this was a rogue male.

No. Recalling the soft noises in the cave, likely this awful-looking creature was a loving mother into whose home I had blundered. Then *he* had come right after me — to attack, she thought, her baby waiting there for her now in the soft darkness. Her counterattack must have flung him headfirst onto the rocks.

Even as I watched, she glided swiftly through the water and flopped into the cave. Only on land was she clumsy. Without wasting another glance she disappeared into the gloom. I was still in danger — terrible danger. I was in a man's boat, dressed in his clothes, and he was dead. I couldn't speak Spanish well enough to talk my way out of this. . . Mexican prisons were not known to be especially nice places.

What was left of my camp would be safe enough until I came back.

I left him floating there without a qualm. John Donne thought that every man's death diminished him. Perhaps it did, but I couldn't regret this man. I pulled the anchor on board and unshipped the oars. As the ship moved away from the sheltering rocks, the wind caught the sail and we began to move with almost frightening speed.

The fishing boats had always gone north, but the wind blew me south. I locked the oars and anxiously searched for a way to control this plunging thing. At last I located a kind of rudder to steer with. South was all right with me. And the sooner the better.

Rounding the edge of the island, I got a shock — there was his big black-and-red boat, bobbing serenely. I threw myself flat in the bottom and steered wide around it. The wind obliged and I swept down the wide, glittering waters, blood-red from the setting sun. There was no shout, no light, no smell of cooking. He must have been alone.

Great jolts of pure joy rocked me as much as the boat's motion and I shouted aloud.

'God! Oh, God!' The first, sheer delight in living that I'd ever felt. *'Thanks!'*

Hours later a small island loomed ahead and I steered for it. In the starlight, it seemed to be as arid and barren as my own island, but totally without birds. That was strange — so crowded on one small place, nothing on another. I hoped there would be no-one to come looking for a missing boat.

Afraid to take down the sail for fear of never being able to put it up again, I pulled into a tiny bay of high rocks and stealthily lowered the anchor. Who knew how far a sound travelled over water? There was food, a badly needed bucket, even a flask of coffee — still hot. I hoped Juan Jose had half as much. I drank it gratefully, never expecting it to keep me awake — and it didn't.

Before the sun was really up, I left. Hours holding the tiller left my fingers raw, till I realised the steering mechanism could be tied in place. I used the sinister little ropes for that.

The boat was a little beauty. We fled along an empty coast, past islands where birds with blue feet nested. Twice dolphins raced alongside, then disappeared, to surface with wide grins an hour later. Brown birds with huge beaks — pelicans? — hitched rides and then flew off. Groups of sea lions lolled past on their backs, waving gentle flippers. I shouted cheerfully to them and laughed at their antics.

I stayed near the shore, but far out in the deep water whales leaped up. They'd land with a tremendous *cr. . . aack!* that foamed the sea. Finally, I began to recognise smaller islands we had seen on the first days of the cruise.

At night I hid in coves and knelt before the God I'd never known. By day I sailed and ate and sang his praises.

One morning in the early mist I saw a gigantic black thing shaped like a bat come straight up out of the ocean. It hung for a second, an enormous nightmare in the fog, then slid back without a sound. It might have been a huge stingray.

At last I reached La Paz.

I remembered the busy pier and drove the ship clumsily into the dock we'd started from. No-one bothered with me. La Paz is a bustling town, used to odd tourist types. Even ones barefooted like me and wearing outsized men's clothes. Probably thought it was the newest trend.

I had no money. I walked for almost an hour before I located the fancy hotel where we'd stayed for one night, waiting for the yacht.

They spoke English. They were polite, though incredulous at first. When they were convinced, there was nothing that they did not do for me. Telephone calls were made, embassy people were informed. I was supplied with a room, a bath, a bed. But most amazing to me was their genuine warmth and pity. I had been nothing to them; suddenly I was wrapped in sympathy, even affection. It took me quite by surprise.

Clothes that fitted were there when, after twelve solid hours, I woke up.

So were *la policía*. Two very professional detectives, one of whom spoke excellent English, took me through the story.

I had done some editing during the long trip back.

'And you landed on Birds' Island?' the older, moustached one wanted to know. *'Isla de Pájaros?'*

'Yes, but we were very weak — from the shock, you know, and all of us kept drifting in and out of consciousness.' I had decided to eliminate the reason we hadn't asked for help. After all, I certainly couldn't identify any of the fishermen and I preferred to keep the leader out of it altogether. The bird killing must be stopped, but I held no grudge against the other men.

'We crawled up near some rocks. One night I heard voices, but I thought it was a dream. Then, the next morning, the eggs were all smashed and there was nothing to eat. We had a hard time.' That was true enough.

'It seems that,' the moustached one paused and continued reluctantly, 'from islands nearby, the people come to steal the eggs. They think to catch the magic.' His scorn was evident.

'But,' I said in a slow, puzzled way, 'these eggs were not stolen. They were *destroyed*.'

The men looked uncomfortable and made getting-up-to-go motions.

'Wait!' They reseated themselves. My father would have issued commands, my mother would have flirted and coaxed. Not my ways. But I needed their cooperation. I tried honesty.

'I must find the man Juan Jose de Gonsalvo. And I must know about the birds.'

The younger man scribbled the few facts. . . his name, the ship, dates, while the older man described a custom I already knew first-hand: stealing 'magic' eggs.

Except for one little nagging detail.

In return, I gave him my version of the rescue. Why wasn't I picked up? Several times I held my head, as if I were dazed. . . they were very sympathetic. 'When I left to search for water, I must have fainted. When I woke up, the rescuers were gone. All I could see was a faraway boat. No-one saw me waving.' So I separated myself from a dead body. Let them find out why he'd left his black-and-red boat.

'And you escaped, how?' This detective was nothing if not thorough.

'I saw a little boat and swam out to it. I waited.' Careful here. 'There was no-one on board. I will be happy to pay the owner.'

Quickly, I changed the subject. 'Look, when you find Juan Jose, I want to know. I owe him a lot.' Moustache looked up. 'It appears to me, *Señorita* Morrison, that you owe him nothing. You did what you could. . .' His voice trailed off.

I persisted. 'I want to know if he's been cared for; I'll pay for his medical expenses.' They nodded. 'And I want to know how to stop the egg-breakers.'

They conferred together in rapid-fire Spanish. 'It is a possibility to notify the societies of animals. . .' the younger one offered tentatively, '. . .before the men come back.'

'But these birds are your national treasure,' I went on, stubbornly. 'Surely there are those who preserve that?'

They looked at each other and shrugged. More rat-tat-tat Spanish. I intended to add that to my list of things to learn. No-one would ever talk over my head again. Finally, they informed me that the navy would be notified.

And now the crucial question. 'What did you mean, they'll come back?'

'Our navy will stay nearby till the eggs come and for a week after, *señorita*,' they told me, 'then they are no more needed.' The younger one stared at me curiously. 'Why you care?'

'Because those birds will be my future.' And there it was, clear as a call. 'One last thing — no, two.' They sighed deeply. 'Tell me the name of some society here in Mexico or the United States where I can talk to somebody. Why save the birds this year and then lose them next year? Right? And finally. . .' I hesitated. 'You said the navy would wait a week. Why a week?'

'The eggs are not good after that, *señorita*,' said the younger man.

'That is why the men come two times,' the other detective added. 'Break the eggs so the birds all lay the second eggs at the same time. The next trip they come to steal.'

I was exasperated. 'But why not steal them twice? Sell the first batch, come back and sell the second batch?' The two men looked at me patiently.

'Even magic eggs no good,' the younger explained, 'if no fresh.'

I gaped at them. 'They killed all those beautiful birds. . . they're wiping out three species. . . just so the eggs would be fresh?' They nodded. We gazed at each other in sorrow.

And abruptly the atmosphere changed.

We weren't adversaries, foreigners or officials any longer; we were more like. . . comrades. And after a small hesitation, Moustache wrote a name for me: Direccion General de Fauna Silvestre, then added: Arizona-Sonora Desert Museum.

'My country, your country — we save the birds.'

'For all the world,' I agreed.

We shook hands, grinning at each other: Quixote, Rosinante, Sancho. Then they became serious, patted my hand, consoled me over my loss, said I could go home whenever I wanted. They hoped that this would not make me unsympathetic towards Mexico.

'A marvellous country; I'll be back,' I assured them. 'The island was beautiful.'

The younger man looked at me uncomprehendingly. 'That island of birds in the Sea of Cortez?'

'Yes,' I told him, 'that island.'

They took their leave doubtfully, as if afraid I was becoming delirious.

I stretched and went to the mirror. A different person looked out at me: tan and slim with rough-skinned hands and black-and-blue bruises all over her legs. The new clothes fitted perfectly. I had not missed the admiration in their eyes.

The 'me' inside was a different matter. Could the whiny fat girl take over again? Yes, she probably could. Would I ever be able to work through — not grief, but at least some understanding for my parents? To give love and accept it, some day? To bring Gran to this pretty little, friendly little place?

I needed a lot of help to find my way. The sense of unfinished business was very strong. Of all the people, I was left alive. Why? *Why?*

I went down to the front desk where they clucked and fussed over me. What could they do to assist me? Anything — anything at all?

'Where's the nearest church?' I asked. With no amazement or amusement, they gave me exact directions and I took my first step forward.

Isla de Pájaros *exists today as a migratory bird sanctuary in the Sea of Cortez off the coast of Mexico. One hundred thousand birds — Heermann's gulls, Royal and Elegant terns — breed there from March to June each year.*

The cooperative efforts of the US and Mexican governments, as well as the students who observe and study there, protect the three species.

The enviromental groups responsible include:

Direccion General de Fauna Silvestre
Audubon Society
University of Mexico, Institute of Biology
Arizona-Sonora Desert Museum
California Academy of Sciences
Nature Conservancy International

*   *   *

Endnotes:

1. 'Suicide's An Alternative/You'll Be Sorry', Frontier F.L.P. 1011, You'll Be Sorry Music, American Lesion Music, 1983

2. 'Memories of Tomorrow,' *ibid*

3. 'Fade to Black', Ride the Lightning, Elektra/Asylum 60396–1, Creeping Death Music, 1984

Harkaran
Dhillon

y5y

10 years old